MOXIE

MOXIE

ALEX POPPE

TORTOISE BOOKS

CHICAGO, IL

FIRST EDITION, April, 2019

Published in the United States by Tortoise Books

www.tortoisebooks.com

ASIN: XXX
ISBN-10: 1-948954-02-8
ISBN-13: 978-1-948954-02-0

This book is a work of fiction. All characters, scenes and situations are either products of the author's imagination or are used fictitiously. Any resemblance to actual events or locales or persons, living or dead, is coincidental.

Cover image and design by Jaime Harris

PART ONE

Bet you'd like one, huh? Sucks to be you. I'll eat the whole fucking bag if I want to. Today is I-don't-give-a-fuck-day, so stop looking at me. Sit somewhere else. You're blocking my view.

One point one million people ride the New York City subway every day, and it feels like half of them are here right now in this car on the Brooklyn-bound L. Hipsters packed in so tight their beards are meshing. NPR says if you have a beard, you have a better chance of getting a job in IT. That's real good news for women.

How long before that guy rocking the Supreme tee and sag-ass skater bottoms cups that Puerto Rican-Asian girl's *culo*? She's a melting pot jackpot. Those PR curves with that Asian skin. I believe her advertising. Look at them talking, teeth chattering in love. I think it will happen as we go through the East River Tunnel. I'll bet you the rest of these Reese's Peanut Butter Cups. Unless you're one of those artisanal craft chocolate fucks on your way to Mast Brothers. What have you got for me?

Damn he's slick. We're not even at First Avenue. I give them six weeks, tops. Then he'll realize she sounds like a wife-magazine article, or she'll experience his pettiness. Everything fresh has a shelf life.

Jesus that bitch there is loud. No one pushed her and now she's acting like just because she lost the genetic lottery, the world is conspiring to make her shitty little life just a bit more miserable. We should stick everyone who is fucked off with the world into a huge wave pool until they remember how to like themselves again. I'd be the first one in.

It's hot. That guy with the origami belly is panting like he's going to expire any minute. Would you offer assistance? One of my exes is a paramedic. He's like an Abercrombie & Fitch model with a little Michael Pitt thrown in for some downtown edge. Can you imagine some rom-com setup where you've been kicked curbside like some recycled fuck-toy, and you wake up to his ruby reds blowing the breath of life back into you? Eyes click in mutual recognition, and there's this moment of heart courage, and you dare to believe in a better version of yourself. Then six weeks later, see above.

The better version of myself is lounging rooftop poolside at King & Grove Lifestyle Hotel drinking Perrier-Jouët with the tooth fairy. Kissing distance to the sky, I am kind, I am beautiful, I am whole. My right cheek is not the texture of crunchy peanut butter, nor is it singed dark like chocolate coating. I do not snap the rubber band on my wrist until pain-darts pierce my skin, shrapnel tearing. I am half-dark, half-light: two-faced when turned-cheek. A yes-no face. If a bullet is a mouthful of pennies, how much is shrapnel?

The train sighs as it slinks into the belly of the Bedford Avenue station. The doors open and close like heart ventricles pumping damp air into the car. A rat races down the subway steps reaching the platform just as the doors close. The train resumes its forward motion. Arms and legs enwombing her cello, a busker on the platform adds a touch of grace to the cacophony of man and machine. A pig-tailed toddler in her father's lanky arms points in my direction and cries. Ditching the bag of Reese's in the trash, I surface at street level behind Supreme tee and PR-Asian hybrid. Together they walk, a tangle of curves and limbs, toward the residential section of Greenpoint. Their cut-out forms shrinky-dink into the lazy chaos of storefront pubs and crowded taco trucks. Sweat slides into the bowl of my back.

Is it cheating or using or just the shit that happens when you yell out someone else's name during sex? What if your partner has had half her face singed and shredded? Can you ask her to wear a bag over her head, or to turn it so only her good side shows? Do you do her from behind or do you leave her behind? Can you lose life-luggage?

Snap, snap, snap goes the rubber band against my wrist. Snap, snap, snap turns my wrist hot numb. Snap, snap, snap hatchets red lines across blue veins. Breathe. This stretch of Bedford Avenue has more missing person fliers than it used to. We are a generation of lost people. What happens to their Facebook pages? I never recognize anyone from these posters, but that doesn't stop me from looking into the eyes on the building sides. Permission to stare granted. I will probably never have gentle sex again.

The abandoned girdle factory on Bedford has been converted into a Premiere Retail Destination so trust fund babies feel ethically consumptive as they pay way too much for pre-torn shirts. Next door is an animal shelter housing other orphans of the city. I have already decided on a dog. It's that one. The one with the black eye in the white face. My muzzle nuzzles her neck. She smells like snow. Blotting my eyes on her fur, I feel her heartbeat pulse against my nose. It is tiny. She is fragile. We are scared. Holding her eye to my eye, her nose to my nose, she licks at my mouth. Head on, she does not turn away. Moxie.

After leashing Moxie, we head toward the skeletal buildings that line the waterfront. Moxie sticks her butt up and waves it like the Queen's hand as she walks. There used to be raves here before some developer realized this section of Brooklyn was worth something and pushed the Poles north, the Puerto Ricans east, and the hookers out. A Vietnam vet with graying dreads photographed tourists in Rock Center by day and squatted here by night. He once gave me a white rose sandwiched between two red ones—said it reminded him of my smile—while we were waiting on the subway platform. Then he asked me for dinner. Moxie's ears prick at the bleating of a foghorn from somewhere along the East River. I don't do dinner.

Back in my apartment, Moxie pees the hard wood on entry. Her tail thumps the floor like she owns the place. Fuck nuts! I'm out of paper towel. There's not even a *New York Times* to wipe it up. I don't relish the thought of piss-soaked toilet tissue lodged under my fingernails. Stashing her in the bath, I start rummaging—which is how I find them lazing under some old tear sheets. That Victoria's Secret

Holiday ad. That ad was... The rubber band bites my wrist. The rubber band breaks. If a bullet is a mouthful of pennies, how much is shrapnel? Fucking useless writing it all down, saving it all up. Where do memories go when you die? Finally these old journal pages are good for something. Hello yellow puddle.

Tomorrow. Is. Really. Happening!!! I get on my first plane. The test shots were great. I don't have to go to school for TWO WEEKS because of this shoot. There is talk of maybe the summer in PARIS. I hope Mom lets me go. I so can't wait for life to start. I hate school. I hate New Jersey. Creepy Mr. Motts is always writing little notes on my lab reports. In biology, all the boys were snickering every time Mr. Motts said penis because it sounded like benis. He can't say his p's!!! Then Ryan Huff asked if the only time the stuff came out was to make a baby. Everyone knows that he and Caitlin Kec are already doing it. He just wanted to mess with Mr. Motts, but it backsplashed on me because Mr. Motts coughed a lot and said no. Sometimes it comes out when you are alone. He was looking at ME when he said it. I think other people saw because I heard snickering, and then my cheeks went all hot. Shit, I hear Mom crying. Steve Jacek asked Simone Brown to sit on his face when Mr. Motts was explaining a diagram of lady parts, and then he called Simone Brown Six-Pack-Simone and all the basketball players laughed. What's so funny about beer? I didn't get it but I pretended to.

The photographer at the test shoot (his name is Jeff☺) wanted to know if I was at least sixteen. I sort of lied and said yes. It's only a lie for the next twenty-three days. He looked down and smiled at his camera when I answered. Then he told me to look at him, not the camera, and then he moved closer and closer shooting film the whole time until we were like six inches apart, just looking at each other. Everything went still. It was like permission to stare, to really look at each other. And then he took the tips of his fingers and brushed them against my left cheek and told me I was so beautiful. I swear I didn't breathe once the whole time. My cheek still feels tingly where he touched it. Mom tells me I'm beautiful all the time but this was different. This time I believed it.

'Moxie,' I call, freeing her from the bathtub. She likes being scratched behind the ears. 'Let's go.' It's Miller time.

✱

'Kaifa.' I greet Alat, the bartender. He was a child soldier in Somalia and looks at all my face when he talks to me. Most people pick a side: stare at the right in disgusted sympathy or stare at the left in concentrated politeness.

'Marhaba habibi. Hamdullah. Kaifik,' which is his standard reply: Welcome dear, I am good, praise Allah. How are you?

'Hamdullah.' Alat knows that's as far as my Arabic goes: handler greetings. 'Do you mind if I bring my dog in?' Moxie is already inside, running the leash around my ankles, but I am not a total twat when it comes to niceties. She rocks her butt from side to side at Alat. How could he resist? Good dog.

'Is it trained?'

'Yes!' I say as I shake my head no. 'But she just peed on my floor so I think we're good for a while.'

'Better take it into the beer garden.'

'Is there air conditioning?' I deadpan. Being spoiled dies hard.

Alat gives me a *look*. 'What's its name?'

'Moxie.' I untangle my feet from her leash to introduce them. 'Alat, Moxie. Moxie, Alat.' Moxie licks and licks the three leftover fingers on Alat's right hand. He doesn't talk about how he lost the other two and I don't talk about how I lost half my face. It's our unspoken pact. Shit, I need to feed her. It's been a while since I've had to think about anyone except myself.

'The usual?'

'And chase it with a beer. It's still hot outside.'

The beer garden is half-crowded. A few heads turn. *Is that...? No, it couldn't be. Jesus! What happened to her?* Imagining the questions is like going to your own funeral. When people can't believe their eyes, they are looser with their tongues.

Shit. I know that girl in the corner rocking the baby carriage. She was an up-and-comer like me until a bad coke habit flushed her down. Her nostrils look red and chapped from where I'm sitting. Good luck, kid.

Alat arrives with my drinks and a bowl of water for Moxie. 'Thanks.' She gulps it down and starts licking my toes. 'You don't happen to have any food she can eat.' I turn my head so only my good side shows and give Alat my cover girl smile.

That's what he sees. From the sidewalk opposite the beer garden. And that's what draws Abercrombie-and-Fitch-with-a-bit-of-Michael-Pitt to the beer garden's perimeter. The smile of my former self. I can almost hear his tumbleweed whispered 'Jax?' as he approaches. My palms itch.

'Jax. I can't believe it. It is you. Stay right there. I'm coming in.' At the sound of my name, Coke Nose gasps in my direction. I subtly thumb my nostrils in return.

'Alat, another please,' and shoot back my Black Label.

This is stupid. I can't sit in profile the whole night. I usually hiss at people when they point at my face. He's not going to point. I have about ten seconds to decide on a strategy. No seconds. Here he is holding a beer.

He's so beautiful it hurts to look at him. His lips are the color of red gummy bears, and cushiony. His skin is so smooth you want to trace it with your fingertips. Looking up at him, I feel less than who I am. Shake it off, girl. Turning my head, I look straight at him and cock my right eyebrow.

He doesn't outwardly flinch. As a paramedic, he's probably used to seeing gruesome sights. My heart beats in my ears. Moxie breaks the silence with a few soft barks. 'Who's that?' He sits down and reaches for her under the table.

'Moxie.' Moxie licks his fingers savagely. She's got good taste.

'I think she's hungry.' He wipes his hand on his jeans.

Moxie resumes licking my toes.

'Yeah,' I feel like my insides are made of glass. This is such a bad idea. 'It's great to see you Aaron.' What do you say to someone you loved two years and half a face ago?

'You don't live above Tops Grocery anymore. I've rung your doorbell a few times.'

This is news. 'Not for a while.'

His phone rings, and from his side of the conversation I gather he lives with his girlfriend, and they share the complexities of domestic cohabitation. It's a far cry from his being shirtless and pantless, standing in my kitchen making cowboy coffee. He's such a grown-up now.

'Sorry about that,' as he shuts off his phone.

'It's all good.' The Black Label and beer and the dying heat are taking effect. Everything is floating.

Aaron laughs to himself. 'I saved that Victoria's Secret ad.'

I don't hide my surprise. 'Why did you ring my ex-doorbell?' Aaron had made me his ex-girlfriend. The Victoria's Secret Holiday ad was the beginning of our end.

'I missed you.' He looks at my good side and places his hand over mine. His calluses rub against my knuckles. He must still lift weights. He leans in closer. 'Can I ask what happened?' He smells like the ocean coated with honey.

You can. But answering requires another round. Alat pokes his head into the beer garden. Hold up two fingers and circle them twice. Make mine a double and everything nice.

'I was on a shoot in Marrakesh. We made a last-minute stop at the souk. A motorcycle bomb went off.' He waits. 'Near where I was standing.' How much more do I need to explain? Half my face is worth a thousand words.

An eruption of laughter peels through the beer garden. Aaron leans closer, the beer mixing with the sweet smell of his breath. 'I'm sorry. I didn't know.'

The sweet breath of a sweet man in a sweet world.

'Thank God it wasn't another 9/11.'

Does bloodshed only count when it is American?

As he shakes his head, his tragedy sympathy falls by the wayside. 'What do the doctors say?'

What do doctors say about cancelled modeling contracts? I finger my rubber band. Right now, I'd settle for drinks out, hold the stares. It's fucking funny: after a lifetime of look-at-me, I wish I were invisible. What do wishes look like?

'They don't say much.' Which isn't exactly true. They said a lot when I was there this afternoon. They said I could do a ton of plastic surgery and maybe I'd come out looking like a comic book character or maybe like someone I resembled. But not like me. 'I don't want to end up the female equivalent of Mickey Rourke.'

This comment earns me a half-smile. 'Same old Jax.' He caresses the top of my hand.

Not really.

'There are so many surgical advances today. Don't give up hope.' He sounds like a cross between an inspirational speaker and an infomercial. My hand sweats under his palm. I don't want pity.

'Yeah, you're right. *Face/Off* was practically a documentary.' I take my hand back.

He looks into my good eye. Freeze frame. 'You were so beautiful.'

The world goes silent.

I was a lot of other things too. No one ever saw them.

The smell of sunbaked pavement wafts through the garden. We empty another round as the sun empties from the sky, banding it blue, green, yellow. I need. To touch. I need to fuck. It's weird to miss someone you are sitting with. Aaron has to go. If I could give back three things to make him stay, I'd give back vintage champagne, all my stays in luxury hotels, and that Victoria's Secret Holiday ad. That ad was everything.

'It was great seeing you, Jax.'

Why do I think I will never see him again? 'You too, Aaron.' My words are soggy. And just like that, he is gone.

✳

I smell it before I see it. Can't see anything behind the big bag of supplies I'm carrying. Was feeling accomplished that I remembered to buy Moxie-necessities on the way home before the smell of dog piss bitch-slapped me across the face when I opened my front door. At least Moxie skirts the puddle instead of running through it. I follow her lead. It's easier than cleaning it.

Moxie noses my calves as I fill her bowl with dog food and set it near her impatient tail. 'Sorry for the wait.' Pour myself a Black Label and sit to watch her eat. Doggie gulping noises permeate the kitchen. 'Slow down girl. A lady picks.' I don't pick. I point. At junk food in supermarkets or bakeries. I look and point and pretend I am going to eat something delicious, something bad for me. Sometimes, looking is enough. At least I'm not a puker like some models. I went to the souk that day to look at the dried fruits in the spice market. Wanted to point at rings of pineapple and wedges of mango and garlands of dates. Wanted to pretend I was going to eat them.

Moxie settles herself by my feet. She looks at me with these wide-open eyes. There's a lump pushing up my throat, and I am tempted to kick her. Her blind trust fucking pisses me off. Grabbing my drink, I open the kitchen window to sit on the fire escape. The night hushes.

The sky has gone inky. From its depth, a single star watches. Looking at my reflection in the kitchen window, I see a faceless girl staring back at me. I want to wake up in her body. There's a hard, blank feeling inside me. I should sleep. When I was an up-and-comer, I never slept. Didn't want to miss anything. It's different now.

The sheets are cool as I slip in between them. Fucking hate sleeping alone. I sleep on only half the bed. Used to love it, back in the day when there were a lot of admirers. Back then, I needed the quiet. Now the quiet riots. Rewind and rewrite tonight as my fingertips stroke my stomach. I am not a boyfriend thief, so in my version of reality Aaron does not have a girlfriend who lives with him. My fingertips tickle up to pinch my nipples. My tits are full, my nipples erect. He says I *am* beautiful, not was, because he sees past the candy shell. Because he misses parking lot salsa lessons and being read to in the bathtub. My hand slides down. Inside I am smooth and slippery. I roll over and grind my pelvis. Pictures flash – Jeff's cock, sucking Aaron's bottom lip, some guitarist's head between my thighs. Tongues pushing more and more and more. My pelvis hooks. An extended present tense. I taste the pillow with my grimace. My body slackens. The ability to speak returns. There is the static noise of silence. My pillow smells sad. I miss so much: middle-of-the-day sex and lying face to face sharing a pillow. Fuck, I miss resting my cheek against my hand. The pillowcase irritates. I turn over toward the window. The sky has lightened. Four black birds fly in a diamond formation against a white sky. How do they stay together? Even lovebirds get divorced. Flying is a cool superpower, but I would choose instant regeneration.

My mouth tastes the way the front hallway smells. Fucking need to take care of the Moxie mess. Like now. I am on my hands and knees with paper towels and piss-soaked journal pages before breakfast. Living the life. Fuck, I miss maid service. That was a great perk of living in model apartments. The agency puts five young hopefuls in a too-small space, competing for the same jobs, and expects them not to kill each other. There is always an odd number of housemates: provides a built-in moderator. I lived in one in Paris. Between the hair-pulling and the tears, there were some moments.

Vive Le Paris! Jeff came over for a visit. All the other girls are like mad in love with him. Who wouldn't be? He's like totally hot and nice and cool and 24! Plus, French Vogue just hired him. And he likes ME! He says he like "discovered me" and he's real proud of it. Mom would FREAK if she heard that because she was my first agent. Anyway, I don't care because it is summer, and I'm in PARIS, and the night sky goes on forever, and I'm in love!!! I haven't said it yet or anything because I'm not like totally stupid, but it's love.

On Friday nights parades of people skate around the Canal Saint Martin. We usually watch them from our balcony. Zaina and Elena (Zaina is from Beirut and has the best hair. Elena is from Kiev and is the skinniest.) got booked on the same shoot and bought us all blades! (They had ten pages of editorial for Italian Elle! Jealous ☹) I haven't scored anything as big, but I feel like it's coming. On Monday I have a go-see for some Pirelli calendar. Whoever that is. Anyway, we drank some Voov Cli Co champagne, donned our skates, and off we went. It was electric. The five of us held hands as we skated, a daisy chain of pretty girls. Nobody was elbowing each other out. I feel like we'll be friends forever.

But the really big news is this. Wait for it ☺. Jeff and I. Hee hee hee. I was really scared because I knew it would hurt, but Jeff was really gentle and patient and like showed me what to do. I was so embarrassed that I didn't know, but I think he got off on that. That he could make me the way he wanted. I finally feel like I belong to someone.

Jesus Fuck.

There is the clip-clip-clip of tiny paws behind me. The soles of my feet receive a tongue bath. 'Morning Toe Licker,' Picking up Moxie, I breathe my dragon breath in her face. She barks. 'Let's go buy a ball.'

Fuck, that sun is bright. Moxie has decided to take her morning dump in front of the entrance to the Brooklyn Fleas. She has no shame. Of course not. She's not the one bent over, picking up warm squishy dogshit with a sandwich baggie.

'Jax! I'd recognize you anywhere,' a voice addresses my ass. 'Girl when did you get a dog? You can barely take care of yourself.'

'Yesterday.' Turning around, I spy Frieda's locks before I spy Frieda. Everything on Frieda has been added: hair, fingernails, breasts. She's a trannie makeup artist with an identical twin brother named Frank. I wonder how long it took for their mother to stop calling 'Boys...' when she wanted both of them. 'This is Moxie. Moxie meet Frieda.' Frieda's one of my few before and after friends.

'How you feelin'?' She takes my chin and turns my face to look at both sides. Her silver bangles jangle. 'Did you see the doctor I told you about?'

She gets away with touching my face because of her six-inch height advantage. And because she was on that Marrakesh shoot. 'Yeah. Yesterday.' I wriggle free. She was having tea with a carpet seller at the hotel at the time of the blast. She visited me almost every week during my recovery to give me a mani/pedi. No one asked her to.

'Girl, you look like shit. Even for you.'

Can't argue with that.

'When's the last time you ate?'

'This morning.'

'Liar.'

She's right. 'So don't ask.'

'Want to have brunch?'

'Can't. I have shit to do.'

'Right. Like you're so important.' Frieda never sugarcoats it.

'Fuck you. I have to get Moxie a ball.'

'So get her a ball after. Girl, starving yourself to death is going to take a while. ODing is much quicker.'

'Fuck you. I don't starve myself.' Besides, I've already decided on hanging. If I were to.

'Fuck you.' Frieda sounds like a junior high cheerleader. 'Fuck you.'

I don't sound that whiny.

'Fuck you-ou.' Frieda's bopping about as she sings it. 'Fuck youuu. Hoo-hooooo.' She grabs my hands and makes me dance along with her, snapping my rubber band. 'Class bling. Let's go to Meatballs. You can drink your lunch. Like Moxie, I need me some balls in my mouth.' Frieda's laugh sounds like a delicious secret.

Bending down to ruffle Moxie's fur, I hide my smile. Sometimes it's easier to give in.

*

After brunch, liquid and otherwise, Moxie and I stroll through McCarren Park. Frieda has a date. Dating – more like snacking. I don't know why Frieda appointed herself my fairy godmother, but I am grateful. She's hooked me up for a prop styling gig next week, which is good because I need something to do.

What the fuck am I going to do with the rest of my life?

Me: *Hi. Is this Lost and Found? I've lost my way.*

Lost and Found: *Have you checked the places you were? You probably left it there.*

Me: *I can't go back to where I was. They won't let me in like this.*

Lost and Found: *I know. Look, it'll turn up. I always find my iPhone at the wine bar across the street from my apartment.*

Me: *Can you just look? It's shiny gold and leads to the top.*

Lost and Found: *Aren't you special? Those are one in a million. Yeah, no. It's not here. You should have taken better care of it in the first place.*

Me: *But, it's not my fault it's gone.*

Lost and Found: *Isn't it?*

Me: *Look, do you know where I can buy a new one?*

Lost and Found: *Do I look like Information? Kindly step aside Ma'am. You're holding up the line.*

Shit, my rubber band is gone. That bitch must have lifted it during the "Fuck You" dance. Despite her Emily Post posture, Frieda's always had sticky fingers.

An African drum ensemble starts up on the far side of the park, grabbing Moxie's attention. She's strong when she wants her way. A small group of people gather around the musicians, dancing. I recognize Jules playing a modest drum near the center of the cluster. Jules is a protest artist whose big moment came when Jay-Z bought one of his paintings. That moment went. Jules' hands slap the drum skin, his long, thick fingers splayed. Feeling a tickle rise between my legs causes me to look away from his lapping fingers. I dated Jules for a minute, a lifetime ago.

'Hey, do you want to dance?' An unfamiliar voice calls from behind.

I turn toward it and fix on a face volcanic with acne. Glittering eye contact. 'Sorry, I have to go.'

✳

Back home, I feed Moxie and sit with my friend Johnnie Walker. I need to kiss someone in the worst way. To put all of who I am into lips and tongue and touch. Kissing is underrated because it's all about the before. People rush that. They don't get that kissing is hope.

Who am I kidding? I need to lose myself in a good lay. Shut out thought and time and place for however long intense foreplay and a heroic orgasm last. I swear, I am ready to call an escort service and order a totally hot guy who stares not and sexes sweet. Not like the last hookup who grabbed a pillow to smother me as I came, and then squirted in my face as he lifted the pillow. I choked and he laughed. Like I wasn't a real person. To him, I was only the shape of one. I don't expect breakfast, but some people are too rough to fuck. It's a fine line deciding whose standards are low enough. Like it fucking matters. In the dark you become whomever they want. Then in the end, you're left with who you are. Jesus mother fucking Christ! I can't stand it inside my head.

With nowhere to go, I go to Alat's.

Sans Moxie, I sit at the air-conditioned bar and watch Alat work. He doesn't say much to anyone. He's probably killed people. How he does not drink the entire contents of the bar baffles me.

'I feel you watching me.' Alat has his back to me polishing glasses. Must be his child soldier instincts kicking in.

'No, I'm not.' I smile like a receptionist at his back.

'Why are you always here alone?' He picks up a knife and starts cutting lemons.

'I'm not always alone. Yesterday I had Moxie.' And Aaron, sort of. 'You're always here alone. Why doesn't your girlfriend ever visit you?' Figure girlfriend is the safer bet.

'My wife is at home with our sons.'

Eights words tell me more about him than half as many months of patronage. Where's his ring? 'Did you meet her here?'

'Muslim women do not usually frequent bars.'

Who knew he was religious? 'Did you know her from Somalia?'

'She knows about my past.'

'That's not what I was asking.' Of course, I deny it.

'Then what?'

That lump is back, clogging my throat. What I really want to know is how he put himself back together. Half-true. I want to know how to put myself back together. Johnnie Walker isn't telling.

'Jax, it's time to grow up. You've had so much more than most.' Alat's eyes are shiny; his voice is not unkind. 'Beauty doesn't feed you.'

Uh, in my case it did. My before-life purls like a junkyard mobile.

'Who are you going to be?'

I have no idea. I used to be so many people.

✱

Twilight hugs the buildings as I walk Moxie along the Williamsburg Bridge. The sky swirls cornflower to carnation as it races the horizon. Looking at it makes my heart hurt in a good way. There is so much beauty above; it makes me feel the tiniest bit alive. The sky was like this in Marrakesh. A color frenzy served up nightly. Thinking about that last day is like touching a hot stove. I last for only so long. It had been my idea to go to the souk. The handler said we needed to get to the airport. I insisted. People don't usually say no to pretty girls.

Purple clouds reef over the East River. All across the boroughs, pretty girls self-decorate and preen in this city of dreams. A leashed figure on four legs pulls a straining figure on two legs around the bottom of Bedford Avenue and heads in our direction. A voice tells Woody to slow down, to heel, but Woody isn't having it. He must have caught Moxie's scent. The two-legged figure turns out to be Heather, a local jewelry designer and sometimes stylist. Jeff bought me one of her pieces, and when I found out about him and Elena (Jax, I zwear it meant nothink. I only did him to get into the *Vogue*), I threw it into the Seine.

Woody reaches his destination and tries to sniff Moxie. She barks and moves away, playing hard to get. But when I reach down to pet him, she charges nose first into his ass. He lets her. Then he tries to mount her. Shit-fuck! I haven't checked if Moxie's been spayed.

'Jax! What a coincidence.' Heather calls as she restrains Woody. 'You're working with me next week. I didn't know you have a dog. Frieda didn't say when we spoke.'

Fairy godmother Frieda must have prepped Heather on my face because it doesn't faze her. 'That's great. Frieda didn't give me the specifics.' Sometimes Brooklyn feels like a village.

'It'll be easy. *Interview* magazine. New York City writers and artists. We probably already have lots of the required items in our personal collections. I'll email you the list.'

People always assume models have tons of shit. When you're starting out, you get paid in merchandise. As you make a name, you get paid in money, a lot of which winds up your nose. Truth is, we wear "borrowed" so often there's no need to buy. *Was* no need to buy. 'I'll look through what I have.'

'Some of us are going to Brooklyn Bowl tonight. There's some Portland band. You should come.'

✴

After Marrakesh I decided it was best not to look at my whole face in the mirror. When I brush my teeth, I usually walk around the apartment dripping toothpaste. If I apply makeup, I parcel my features in a hand mirror. The full-length mirror is propped against the bedroom wall at neck height. Johnnie Walker has encouraged me to try something new. I sneak up on the bathroom.

Don't be such a pussy. Lights on. Fuck, just look at yourself. When you were sixteen you stared into everything reflective. Count of three. Go. Seeing the caulked texture of my dark cheek causes a hot stripe to shoot up my throat. Scabby spackle tracks my right temple and fans above my right eyebrow. Widening my scope, I take in my straight nose and generous mouth. Breathe. My eyes sweep left and up. Dewy, creamy, porcelain skin. Finally, I meet my gaze. Stagnant eyes regard me.

Johnnie Walker you are a tricking Tom-fuckery son-of-a-bitch. The only response is to finish you.

My handler leads me through the souk's labyrinth of stalls. The scents of jasmine and orange blossom flirt with the aroma of chicken shish. Everywhere is Color! Color! Color! Barrels of mustard-yellow saffron, burnt sienna turmeric, and dried red peppers compete with three-foot

Crayola-hued flowers under a candy-blue sky. Somewhere an *oud* plays. My mouth waters for the dried pineapple and mango which hang in slabs above the barrels. The fruit slabs have hinged jaws, which start moving up and down laughing. Their dried-strawberry kebab tongues lash at my hair. I point at the slabs while my handler negotiates the price. 'No,' my lips move as if in peanut butter. I can't form words. My handler turns toward me. Everything quiets to a vibration as a motorcycle pauses down the lane. The vibration grows to a rumble to a thunder to silence as the motorcycle cartwheels apart. A hubcap frisbees through the air. The ground hits me. My face feels like wet fire. Some god unmutes the sound. Under invocations and pounding footsteps, there is doglike moaning flooding with saliva. A siren wails and wails and wails.

The ringing phone wakes me. How the fuck did I end up on the bathroom floor? Stop ringing stop ringing stop ringing. Thank you oh merciful God. My mouth tastes like dry, cracked ass. The bathroom sink helps me stand. The room swivels from side to side. Fucking phone starts fucking ringing again. Jesus fuck, who the hell calls at 3:00 a.m.? It's not like I fucking have fuck buddies. Stumble into the kitchen. No phone, but there is a scatter of dog chow on the floor and a snoring Moxie. Her legs move as if she's running. The ringing stops while I pop some aspirin; it starts again by the time I dump the contents of my handbag onto the living room floor to find my phone.

'Frieda, what the fuck. It's after three.' I feel vomity.

'Girl, where's "hello"? Didn't your mama raise you right?'

Emily Post manners too.

'She raised me not to fucking phone at three in the fucking morning. Look, if this is about–'

'Girl, it's not all about you. I need you.'

FUCK.

'What happened?'

'Just come over.'

What could be a few minutes later, I am panting outside Frieda's apartment door.

'It's about time.' Frieda's butterscotch voice has turned to sandpaper.

Fucking, fucking hell. Her face.

'Girl, is that what you sleep in? No wonder you're attracting degenerates.' She moves to let me in.

'I should have never told you about the Smother-Squirter.'

'Do I look that bad?'

She does. Her left eye is swollen shut and her bottom lip is split. Her wig lies forgotten near the sofa. Her open kimono exposes her hairless flat chest and swollen, knobby ribs. I go into the kitchen to avoid looking at her. Grab an alibi of ice. When I return, Frieda's lying on the couch examining her face in a hand mirror. Most of her fingernails have been broken.

'Girl, is ice all you got? You? That is downright shameful. Go get Mama a tequila. It's much more,' her voice cracks, 'to the point.'

'Frieda—'

'Bring the bottle.'

'Do you want to go to the hospital? I'll go with you.'

Frieda's right eye cuts me. 'Bottle.'

I take the mirror from her hands and lay it on the coffee table. 'Trust me. You don't need this now,' and go back to the kitchen. By the time I return, the mirror has been flung against a wall.

Focusing on the air above her shoulder, I hand her a shot.

'Look at me.'

'I am,' I lie.

'Look me in the eye.'

Stare at her eyebrow.

'I'm never afraid to look at you.'

My face heats. 'What happened? I thought you had a date.'

'It's all fun and games until somebody gets laid. Bastard ran first sign of trouble.'

'I'm sorry.'

'People disappoint.'

'I'm sorry.' There is a subtle rearranging of air. Refresh her ice packs before getting her a blanket and another pillow. Go to put some ointment on Frieda's split lip and she bats my hand away. My hand becomes her speed bag.

'I am so angry.' Her voice drags on my insides.

'I know.'

'Do you?' Her right eye haunts me. 'Who's ever come after you simply for being who you are?'

Fat seconds strobe by. I can't make a home for how she feels. Pull a chair to the sofa and settle in for what's left of the night.

I wake to wet. My forehead is resting on damp sofa cushions next to Frieda's stomach. All the ice packs have melted. Some fucking nurse I am. Head to the kitchen to mix some tequila and OJ for her. She's going to hurt when she wakes.

'Girl, what are you doing in my kitchen? Lord knows you don't know how to cook.'

'Mixing a magic potion.' Down a sly shot before returning. 'Here. Drink this. Then I'll help you shower.'

Frieda wrinkles her nose like I've just farted garlic and cheese. 'Help me what? No.'

'For fuck's sake Frieda. It's not like I haven't seen one before.'

'But mine is spectacular.' A small laugh makes her grabs near her ribs. 'I don't want to ruin you.'

'Little late for that. To your spectacular cock. Cheers.'

'Cheers.' Frieda coughs hard. 'Shit girl.'

'You need to numb yourself. You think you hurt now? You're not even standing.' Frieda takes my comment as a challenge and swings her legs round to the floor, biting back a groan. She gives up and drains her drink. We wait for the tequila effect.

'You hear about this shit, but when it happens to you...'

Hate is a blanket. 'Are you scared?' I top her off.

'Scared of little boys with little pricks and even littler minds? Shit no, girl. Bring it on.' Her face says anything but. With all the wrappings torn away, Frieda looks like someone who's kept one eye over her shoulder her whole life.

'Ready for your sponge bath? It'll be fun.'

'You ever bathe someone? Medically speaking?'

'No, but I once sucked Jeff off as some guy popped his dislocated shoulder back into its socket. Does that count?' Am I exaggerating? Mostly.

Frieda can't tell whether to believe me or not. 'To think all this time, I thought you were a good girl.'

'More like a good slut.' I hold out my hand to Frieda and gently pull her up.

✳

By the time I get home, Moxie has peed the floor again. Can't really blame her. Thank God for Bounty, the quicker picker-upper. I wish they made the equivalent for people.

As Moxie eats I reach for my laptop instead of Johnnie Walker. Seeing Frieda all banged up is fucking with me.

Heather's email is at the top. Scan her prop list. A bullwhip? Really? She'd be better off asking Frieda. Gothic jewelry? Check. Will bring that Peruzzi cross. Hot house orchids? Curious to see who these artists will be. About to log off when a new message pings my inbox.

The name is Arabic so I know who it's from before I open it. Get up and am halfway to the shelf where Johnny Walker lives when the image of Frieda's right eye watching me doctor her cut lip pushes into my mind. Her martini laugh echoes in my empty kitchen. Motionless, I stand listening to Moxie's paws clacking against the tiles. Snap. My wrist smarts. Snap. I go back to my chair and sit down. Mr. Walker's not going anywhere.

Dear Miss Jax,

I hope you is well and your family. I write you for to show you how Layla growing. Me attache the image. The money that you us gave it when Naji was died very help us. Ma Layla in the school. She and me in security. She and me, we have good life.

As-salaam 'alaykum,

Aamina El-Khoury

Aamina was my handler's wife. His name was Naji. I almost never say it. Refer to him as The Handler. But he had a name and a wife and a daughter. Then a dervish motorcycle hubcap spun into his neck and he didn't have them anymore. That moment lives in my head, an always. Condolence payments didn't bring him back. Another thing you can't buy. I pick up Moxie to show her the sweet picture of Layla. Bury my face in her fur. She smells alive. My growling stomach startles us both.

Moxie and I head over to Teddy's Bar and Grill under a dirty sky. Teddy's serves a tequila sampler in case Frieda checks her messages and joins us. I sit at an outside table to watch the world go by as Moxie settles at my feet. Thinking about Aamina's email and the prop gig tomorrow makes me feel lighter. I order a goat cheese burger.

The smell of weed wafts by. It's followed by a tall, skinny dude with dark chin-length hair and a high forehead. His ears are pierced, his goatee trimmed, and his green eyes red. There is something about him that makes me want to run out and get my nipples pierced and my ass tattooed. Even Moxie is distracted from the lure of my toes by this stranger's entrance. Fucking why-oh-why did I wear a lavender sundress? I feel like a reject from a prom dress casting. Shit. He just caught me staring. Shitty fuck. I have nothing to hide behind.

'Hey,' he passes and sits down at the next table. I "hey" back wondering how high he is not to have been freaked out by my face. It's not like I can turn around to check.

Then: 'My Lord girl, is that you in a dress?'

Frieda knows how to make an entrance. She has styled herself like an Amazonian Holly Golightly in oversized dark sunglasses and a little black shift. She sports a diamante clip in her streaked updo and pearls around her neck. 'Glad to see you're feeling better.' Moxie barks her approval.

'Girl, you know you can't keep a good woman down. Not unless she wants to be, and you've been veeery good.' Frieda laughs like I've offered her a Cartier box filled with diamonds and then winces, fingering her ribs. Swagger trumps pain. The waitress appears with my burger. 'Now I've seen it all.'

'I told you I eat.' Just not every day. 'It's not my fucking fault you fucking don't believe me. Want half?'

'Thank God that sentence had at least one "fuck" in it or I'd doubt you were you.'

'No one else has this face.'

'No one else has that body either. And right now, it is being admired by one very sexy stoner.' Frieda leans back. 'Hey-hey at the next table. Were you just checking out my friend's very fine ass?'

I'm ready to stuff my burger into her mouth. A chair scrapes along the sidewalk. Way to go Frieda. Frighten the poor fucker away.

A low chuckle. 'I guess I was.' His voice invites like a bowl of hot chocolate.

'I can't say I blame you,' Frieda says, tipping her sunglasses. 'It's even better bare,' she purrs.

Jesus mother fucking Christ. 'Shut the fuck up!' I hiss, breaking the cinematic inevitability of the moment.

'What? Do you feel objectified?' Frieda deep throats one of my French fries. 'Are you, the model of a Pirelli calendar and two *Sports Illustrated Swimsuit Issue* covers, offended by compliments to your physique?' It is awe-inspiring and a little gross what Frieda's tongue does with food. 'Besides, I think he's enjoying the attention. His Christmas eyes are smiling.'

I shrug my eyebrows in response.

Frieda flags the browsing waitress for a drink. 'You don't understand. You've never been background music.'

'But now I'm a fucking freak show.'

'Even the Elephant Man got laid.'

'Frieda, I'm serious. I miss what I looked like, and I don't care how that sounds.'

'Aren't you more than the sum of your parts?' Frieda's laugh goes from a bell to a drum. 'Now, I may dress up my outside, but I know what's on my inside. Despite the cock and balls, I am one hundred percent woman.' Frieda sings the last word over to Christmas Eyes, smiling with all her teeth.

'You go through a lot of work to be a *pretty* woman. Just last night all those fingernails were broken; today, good as new. Because life is easier for pretty people.' Before Marrakesh, how many times did we get VIP treatment or some impossible freebie because of how I looked?

'Girl, that's trappings. We're all just playing the game for however long we get to play it. What would you have done when you got old?'

I don't know. Before, age was a knock on a faraway door. 'Wait for my professional athlete/rock star husband to cheat on me while I raise our kids upstate? Isn't that what supermodels do?' Truth is, I never thought past the next booking. Before Marrakesh, the bookings seemed like they'd last forever.

'Do you want children? You know, they're harder than dogs.' Her comment stops my feeding Moxie bits of my burger.

Doesn't motherhood have a learning curve? 'I know I am supposed to.'

'Your problem is you don't know what you want because you don't know who you are.'

'Yes I do. I want my old life back. It was so easy. Someone told me where to be and when to be there, and all I had to do was dress up and live in whatever created fantasy there was while someone took my picture.' The conversation waits for me. 'Who wouldn't want that?'

'Some of us want to make our own choices. Your old life was lonely.'

'All life is lonely. That's why people breed.'

Frieda's lips prune. 'That part of your life is over.'

Looking back is prettier than looking at. 'But I like life through the looking glass.'

'You're whining.'

The thought pesters me like a roving itch. When I was beautiful, was I happy? Most of the time, I was moving too fast to be anything. It was fun, but is fun the same as happy? It's been seven months since Marrakesh and I don't remember how happy feels. 'You're a dull ache in the vagina.'

We sip in silence.

*

Moxie and I walk the waterfront desire line of Kent Avenue toward the Brooklyn Navy Yard. I love this old mixed neighborhood with its industrial buildings and scarred cityscape. It's that hour of daylight when you wish you could taste sunshine. A starvation-zone body of a girl, modeling portfolio under her arm, scurries toward the remnants of the Domino Sugar Refinery. She has my hair and eyes, and if I were twelve years younger and just starting out, we'd probably run into each other at the same casting calls. What gets me is her gait; she hasn't taken charge of herself. She'll need to own it if she wants to walk New York, Paris, or Milan.

A beeping horn startles me. What the fuck? A truck painted with Hayman's Handyman Service pulls up alongside me. Christmas Eyes is behind the wheel.

'Hey.'

He likes his one syllable words.

'Hey.' Moxie and I approach the truck. 'What's Hayman's Handyman Service?'

'It's pronounced *high* man and it's my company.'

Hymen? I smother a smile. 'What's your first name?'

'Richard.'

He is straight-faced. It is too much. I have to go there. 'Your parents named you Richard Hymen? Dick Hymen? Do you still talk to them?'

'It sounds different in Hebrew. Do you want a ride?'

'I'm walking Moxie. Riding defeats the purpose.'

'I have a dog near Prospect Park. We could walk them together.'

'How fast can you move? Usually we shit and run.'

'That's not cool.'

A stoner with a conscience.

'I know,' I say as my hand puppetizes the plastic baggie at the bottom of my handbag. Emerging, the bag takes on a voice of its own. 'Feed me,' it growls.

'You're crazy.' He opens the passenger side door and I climb in, with a stranger, who is totally high. Crazy is a sliding scale.

'What's your name?'

'Jax.'

'And you busted *my* balls?'

'My name is cool.'

'I'm sure "Jax" is on your birth certificate.'

'It is!' I lie. I don't cop to Jacinda.

Holding Moxie on my lap, I tell the kind of stories you tell someone who has no idea who you are. I wonder when he'll realize that most of it is bullshit. I'd love to know if he's high enough to sex me. You think about what someone's like when you first meet him.

We pull up to your average pre-gentrified neighborhood triplex. 'This is me.' He parks.

I am suddenly nervous about leaving the front seat. This whole time, he's faced my left side. 'Do you want to get your dog while I wait here?' I watch his slim hips walk away.

Free from the truck, Moxie runs her crazy-dog circles around me. A moment later Richard returns with an ambling tobacco-colored mutt. How much weed does he smoke inside his apartment?

'This is Dean.' Richard bends down to rub Dean's head and neck. He pauses to check the milky film over Dean's right eye and whispers something I can't hear in Dean's ear. Then he steps aside to let the dogs meet. Moxie approaches Dean and sniffs. Dean couldn't care less. Moxie barks and barks at Dean's staggering indifference. Dean turns away to follow Richard.

'That went well. Which way to the park?'

'Follow me.' Richard doesn't bother leashing Dean.

I stay on his right side so from his point of view it seems like everyone walking dogs has a normal face.

When we get to the park, I unleash Moxie. She sniffs at every tree while Dean trails us like an Italian chaperone. 'How old is he?'

'Dean's eleven. What about Moxie?'

I don't know. 'I got her from an animal shelter a few days ago. This dog thing is a bit new for me.'

'Why'd you get her?'

'It's like...you know.' My answer satisfies his stoner logic. 'Why'd you stop me on Kent?'

'I was leaving my dealer's and I thought, there's that girl with the very fine ass.'

'What about the face?' I keep my gaze on the horizon. The light has gone pastel.

'Less fine than your ass.' His answer is an emotional paper cut. 'What happened?'

'Wrong place, wrong time.' I decide to flirt with hurt. 'Do you think a person could ever not notice it?'

He stops walking and turns me toward him. Because little jolts of electricity twist from his fingertips up my arms, I indulge his looking spree. His gaze is honest but not reproachful. My stomach unclenches. 'No. It's hard to look at and hard not to.'

Skin crackling silence.

'Being high helps.'

What are the chances he's high all the time?

'Your friends notice it, but they know you so they probably don't care.'

I think about Frieda. She treats me the same as always. When Heather invited me to Brooklyn Bowl, she didn't seem to care. Did Aaron care?

'You could always drink at vet halls if you don't want it stared at. Next to a serious burn victim, your face would seem minor.'

Comparative attractive suffering – the new reality TV show.

'You don't say much.'

'I'm thinking about what you've said.' It feels like he's shown me the stranger of myself. Am I supposed to be thankful? Does his rockstar appeal outweigh his assholeness? Will he suggest I write to prison convicts next?

'I've seen worse.'

I pull a smile out from some place. Get it right on the second try. It pisses me off when people remind me that others have suffered more than I have. They didn't lose what I lost. 'Where?'

'When I was in the army in Israel.'

'What'd you do?'

'If a bomb went off or there was a firefight, I was on the team that removed the damaged vehicles. We worked near the Lebanese border. We were busy.'

'I was on a shoot in Marrakesh. Insisted on going to the souk. There was a motorcycle bomb.' Those tumultuous, stupid seconds. 'In a way, it's my own fucking fault.'

'No, it's not. Bomb shit is uncool. I grew up with that shit. Bombs in public places all the time.'

I had no idea. Being the product of an American upbringing, my words go into hiding.

'Dude, where's your dog?'

Shit-fuck. It's been a while since I've seen or heard Moxie. Dean sits at Richard's feet like a testimony to Richard's abilities as a pet owner. I thrust the empty dog leash inside my handbag.

'Don't worry. We'll find her.'

I envy his cannabis calm.

'Moxie!' I yell as I run forward. 'Moxie, I've got your red ball. Moxie! Toe Licker. Come out, come out wherever you are!' The fucking trees sing back to me.

Mother-ass bitch! Why can't I enjoy a fucking walk in the park like a normal fucking person without losing my fucking dog? Frieda's right. I can't take care of myself. Who was I fucking kidding getting a dog? I've never kept houseplants. I'm incapable of sustaining anything lasting.

I hear Richard yelling for Moxie in another part of the park. Tree shadows tickle the shrubs as the sun climbs down from the sky. I feel violent toward the park. What looks to be a seven-year-old boy pokes a stick at something under a giant oak. He frolics with the boughs, his mop of curly red hair bobbing up and down as if the leaves answer him. His loose laughter makes me want to slap the joy right out of him. Snap. Snap. Snap. The pain jolts. Snap. My feet move toward him unearthing grasslings. Snap. Maybe he's seen Moxie.

'Whatcha got there?'

Startled, the boy straightens, brandishing the stick like a sword. When he sees my face, he screams and runs helter-skelter, disappearing within the folds of the park's leafy skirt.

'I'm gonna get you. I'm gonna get you. I'm gonna get you.' My voice scratches like jagged tree bark. Fucking brat. Walking fucking argument for birth control. Wish I could fucking shove him back up his mother's hooch. Where he was standing is a brown, chunky puddle with bits of ground pinky sirloin.

Richard and Dean catch up to me. Dean's presence is an accusation. 'Any luck?'

'Maybe. Is that animal or human?'

Richard restrains Dean. 'The way Dean's interested I would say animal. It could be dog puke or diarrhea. Did you feed her any of your lunch?'

I had ordered today's burger medium rare. 'How did you know to come this way?'

'Some screaming kid ran past me. Figured he might have seen you.'

'Fuck you.'

Richard shrugs his shoulders as he hands me a business card. 'Email me a picture of Moxie with contact info, and I'll put up some fliers in the neighborhood. Someone might have taken her home.'

I don't have a single picture of Moxie. I couldn't make a fucking missing dog flyer if I wanted to. I take his card. The sky looks tenuous. Did I say thank you? 'She's probably better off without me.'

'Don't be like that. I've seen the ways she licks your feet. You'll find her.' He squeezes my shoulder. 'Look, I need to get Dean home to give him his eye drops. If you follow the path to the right, it leads toward the lake. Does she like water? Maybe you'll find her there. If you don't find her, send me that picture.' He and Dean head left into the shadows. Our paths diverge: two people going back to their separate lives.

PART TWO

Silence hangs from a poppy-seed sky. Who the fuck gets up this early besides the Mexican cleaners dreaming of fifteen an hour? No morning toe-licking as coffee rinses a bath tub ring of whiskey scum from my mouth. Traces of dog food have dried into skid marks at the bottom of Moxie's bowl. Johnnie Walker cajoles from his throne on the shelf.

Three break dancers commandeer a subway car aisle on the Manhattan-bound L. The smallest one pretzels himself around a support pole, stripper-style, while the other two monster around on their hands along the shoe-printed floor. Their T-shirts slip, revealing housing-project-slim torsos. A woman with Christmas-tree hair tucks money into the waistband of their Calvin Klein briefs.

Above street level, the High Line ribbons its way along the Hudson River into Chelsea. Eyes closed, I head west to Milk Studios. Shot a Victor & Rolf fragrance campaign on the penthouse's roof deck wearing nothing but the bottle ten months ago. My feet take root midway across Fourteenth Street. Fuck of shit. I can't watch a bunch of niche-important people with pornographic lips having their pictures taken. Turn, head back toward the subway. Stop. Turn toward Milk, take a step and stop. My legs feel like they're praying. A taxi screeches down the middle of my hangover.

'Make up your mind sweetheart.'

I look at him with pissy severity.

'Nice face.' He guns it.

Fuck yeah it is.

✳

A slow sun filters through the windows of the loft studio. A second assistant producer totters about on a pair of four-inch Manolos, carrying her extra pounds like an apology. There is a flurry of activity among the surgically self-improved awaiting the talent. Everybody is carefully not looking at me. I age in dog years. Heather arrives with the photographer, a computer-hacker type with warrior cheekbones. His skin has a consumptive sheen.

'Jax, great you're here. Let me introduce you to The Dylan.'

My smile gives nothing of itself. 'Nice to meet you.'

'Perfect.' The Dylan glides us into the stretching daylight. 'Fascinating. The texture. The color. Raw. Carnival. I need to capture it.' His fingers make free with my face. Snowflakes of pain scatter across my cheek and temple. Outside the window, the buildings of lower Manhattan morph into a skyline of liquor bottles. I remember I have arms and give him a hard little shove away. The crowd of suck-ups erupts into a susurrated blather of dime store concern and then quiets for the take down.

'What the fuck?'

'A live wire woman.' The Dylan chuckles like he's gained carnal knowledge. 'Heather, Jax with me. Minions scatter. Talent in ten. People, we have ART to make.' Everyone moves at the speed of a high colonic.

What the fuck just happened? I wish I were in a nameless elsewhere.

Heather manages a skewered smile. We dress the set.

Ten spreads to twenty spreads to fifty and still no talent. This is worse than church. The sky turns the color of cue chalk. Wonder where Moxie spent the night. Was going to look for her after the shoot but cock knows how long this will take. When I was the talent, I was never late for a booking.

The artist scheduled second arrives first, a sculptor who deconstructs world icons and recasts them in copper sections which he scatters across the globe. He'd look more at home behind a supermarket meat counter than he does surrounded by orchids in front of The Dylan's lens. The artist neither moves nor talks, preferring to sit statue-still in a metaphysical doughnut hole. From the sidelines, my back arches, neck extends and chin tips upward as if balancing a shot glass. The Dylan's camera lens becomes a crafty sniper's eye as it swerves in my direction. The shutter machine-guns before The Dylan winks at me and refocuses on the sculptor. Mother-ass bitch. Need to break that fucking camera.

The next artist is a furniture designer who specializes in ballroom light fixtures made of bra cups. One of them hangs in the Whitney. Internationally tan, he has the moneyed style of a Viagra ad. Are those highlights? That bullwhip on the prop list must be for him.

'Has anyone ever told you, you're pretty enough to model?' His voice makes me think of eels. Over my shoulder, Bra Cups is looking at my ass like it's his next bite of hamburger.

'My name is Larry.' Bra Cups turtles up to me. 'I know a few people.'

His breath pollutes the back of my neck.

'This feels like a moment. Does Pretty have a name?' Larry's got the game of a travelling salesman purring pickup lines in an after-hours. How many women have slept with him just to make him go away?

Pivoting, I confront him with my face. Wait as his eyes make a pit stop at my tits and then work their way north. Look at him all warm and gooey. He deflates.

For a moment, I almost like how I look. 'Jax.' Squeeze his hand hard because I can't lift my leg and spray him. Larry winces. I turn my ethics off. Graze my breast against his forearm before releasing his hand. There is the slightest gravitational pull rising from his pants. Disgust and lust slug it out across his face with no clear winner. I haven't felt this in control since that hotel room in Marrakesh. Someday, I hope a man will surprise me.

Larry recovers with dry-cleaned confidence. 'Jax is an interesting name.'

Hope is a timid thing.

'Where does it come from?'

A ten-year-old Larry being reminded to keep his elbows off the dinner table flashes before my eyes. His hard-working, never-home-for-dinner father probably had mistresses. Ten-year-old Larry idolizes his father.

'My father's a gambler.' I use a sad I-love-you voice. Ever notice how people sound like they're suffering when they say 'I love you'? I am the hideous kinky of Larry's anorexic wet dreams. It shows in the "O" of his mouth. He probably has jackhammer sex.

Larry's eyes slide back to my tits. 'There's something so familiar about you. I wish I could put my finger on it.' His hand reaches out. Larry's groan is a rolling river. I am caught in a disgustingly cozy fugue. His eyes pinwheel.

'You've probably rubbed one out to one of my Sports Illustrated swimsuit spreads.' Knock his hand from my breast. My sexually purposed life, abandoned.

'Me and all of male America.'

'Like to think I had female fans too.' I spank him with my voice. Whee!

Larry's imagination spins to the other side and back. The strain in his pants is heroic. 'Yeah?' He sounds like he is drowning.

My cocked brow is a vague yes to his porn-lite hope.

'Do you want—'

No,' it comes out as spiky as I meant.

'There are ways around your face.'

I give him a pigeon's empty stare. I am not less than the sum of my parts.

✱

The day stretches on like a flavorless wad. Around 3pm, I'm sent on a coffee run, which is an opportunity to liberate a shot of Jack from a neighborhood dive. It's got the charm of a wooden barn where people pee in the corners. The bartender's bulbous face belongs on the carved knob of an antique cane. Emitting a fresh beer buzz glow, he slides a bowl of recycled pretzels my way. I used to sip Cristal while someone without thickness in his face did my hair and makeup. It's getting harder and harder to keep on nodding terms with the person I used to be. Another shot numbs my interior out.

Across the bar, a pencil of a woman with hair like an electro-fried poodle reapplies lipstick to the slash of her mouth. Beauty fades, but sex fades faster. These days, is she loved like a stick of gum? Her beauty has curdled. She probably lives in a cluttered one-room rent-controlled walk-up and eats dinner standing over the kitchen sink. How often does she go the whole day without speaking to anyone? A sudden shiver pulls my arms into a one-person hug. Flinging some bills on the bar, I fly to Starbucks, the wind scraping the hair from my face.

Back at Milk, the studio teems with plot and intrigue. A new guy with the casually disheveled look of a foreign correspondent stalks the foreground like he can't remember where he's parked his car. Larry is soliciting bra donations from the sheep of pudding-faced girleens ready to hustle for exposure and notice. When I enter, their soft, snarky laughter is his bonus serving of sympathy. Heather and The Dylan are nowhere in sight.

'Could I get one of those or are they all taken?' New Guy's voice is garlanded in gravel.

'Help yourself.'

'Thanks. What do I owe you?'

Shake my head and stare at the coffee, waiting for it to tell me what to do.

'I'm Lukas.'

Who offers his hand these days?

Lose the tray of coffee and find my tongue. 'Hi. I'm Jax.' Shaking his hand has a campfire intimacy.

'Can I ask you a personal question?'

Fuck. Is asking a question better than ignoring the elephant defecating all over the living room?

'Why is a Victoria's Secret model getting coffee?'

'Is there something on my face?'

'I can see you've had some sort of accident. But why are you getting coffee?'

Is he real or a remarkable imitation?

From the corner of my eye, Larry ties a Cosabella bra around his head and moonwalks with inept abandon. It's impossible not to imagine his hairy pencil-sharpener-shaped asshole. He's worse than reality TV. Take a step towards Lukas to block him from my view. 'I'm helping. What do you do?'

'I'm a journalist.'

'You look like a journalist. Artfully disarrayed.' He probably has an erudite ficus tree in his home office.

'You're funny.'

'Sometimes.' We circle around each other like two dogs getting ready to play. 'What have you written? Or am I supposed to know?'

'The last thing I did was on teenage prisoner abuse at Rikers.'

'So light fluff.'

'Pretty much.'

'I bet you're good.'

'How so?'

That is the question. 'You're easy to talk to. People probably open up.'

'Sometimes.' He ping-pongs the word back to me.

Did he snug a teeny bit closer? I catch his clean outdoorsy smell.

'So Miss Jax, people say I'm easy to talk to. Tell me something true.'

I usually leave out a lot when I tell the truth.

'You first. Tell me your deepest, darkest, most personal intimate secret, and I promise I won't tell anyone.' Cross my heart as I shake my head no. Give him my big eyes.

'OK.' He rummages through his personal mythology. 'Until I was about eleven, I didn't have a dime that I hadn't stolen.'

People are icebergs. 'What happened at eleven?'

'I got a paper route.'

'And thus began your career in journalism.' We toast with our coffees.

'Your turn.'

'I never graduated from high school.'

'You're kidding.'

My answer surprises me too. 'The summer after I turned sixteen, I went to Paris to model and never looked back.'

'Didn't your parents try to stop you?'

'My mother encouraged me.' To put it mildly.

'Do you regret it?'

'Before, I would have said no.' Before stretches. The long white fingers of daylight grasp at air. Snap. Snap. Take a moment of not breathing. 'Now...' Now is an unravelling hem. Modelling is the only way I know myself, but I've become its stalker. 'I don't know what now is supposed to be.'

'That's the thrilling part.'

Does his confidence come from reciting daily aspirations? It's not thrilling: it's falling down an elevator shaft and there's no bottom. I want to tear a hole in myself and flee through it.

'Are you okay?' His fingers feel like a butterfly landing on my shoulder. 'I didn't mean to upset you. I'm sorry.'

I pester the rubber band around my wrist.

'What you need is some *futter für die seele.*'

'What?' His comment pulls me out of my head cinema.

'*Futter für die seele.* Literally soul food. It's German for comfort food.'

I have Johnnie Walker for that. 'Suggesting a model eat is like giving a junkie a full syringe.' Ex-model.

Lukas eye-points at the rubber band. 'You intrigue me, Miss Jax. Maybe you'd let me write about you.' His business card says *The New Yorker.*

The bathroom door flings open and The Dylan emerges smelling like a French accident. Heather trails him, specks of white dusting her nostrils. My mouth waters for some Walker.

'You're here. Good. Follow.' The Dylan pinballs toward the set as Heather starts to DJ. Music scribbles on us.

The bathroom door sighs, exhaling the makeup artist who dances Lukas to her chair.

✳

The sun fattens as it ebbs on the horizon, and the skyscrapers over the Hudson begin to glow. I make my way east across the cobblestone streets of the Meatpacking's defunct S&M club district to the West 4th Street subway station. Add my stench to the spaghetti of people tangled inside the Brighton Beach-bound B train. A penguin of a woman ricochets off my side as the train car hits a track curve, her lopsided smile etching wrinkles into an algebra of skin before it floats off into empty space.

Prospect Park pulsates with activity in the tangerine light. Amidst cyclists, runners and double-wide strollers, two teens exchange kisses on a park bench. The boy, as sloppy as a little cat, traces the bridge of the girl's nose until her cheeks are the color of baby's feet. She laughs fatly at something he says and they shipwreck-kiss again, interlacing their fingers. My sense of presence deserts me until I realize I'm staring like a perverted ventriloquist's dummy. Cross a field toward the lake.

What now? Circle the sixty-acre pond, calling Moxie's name? Fuckety-fuck. She could be anywhere, or drowned like that two-year-old last summer. I become a photograph of myself. Taking a step forward is harder than catwalking for Karl at the Grand Palais. A group of tweens sunbathing in the grass explode into laughter. Hope you get skin cancer, bitches.

Up ahead, a shirtless man with a second-trimester heft breaks the pane of water with his fishing line. His molded locks look like a wave about to crash. At his side, a young boy bends down, his naked torso as simple as a shell, to retrieve a worm from a bucket. He stands, revealing the same shock of hair, before he magics the worm onto a hook and casts his line. Tall and small, they stand in companionable quiet, the boy stealing looks at the man, adopting his stance, mimicking the older man's hypnotized gaze across the water.

As far as I can see, no stray dogs are touting lakeside, giving paws until their dumbass owners find them. A kite writing on the blue above with its red tail becomes my North Star. Farther into the park, a group of onlookers scatter like mice freed from a laboratory. They dart among tree shadows authored by the sun, snapping pics with their smartphones. Images of a mutilated Moxie kaleidoscope through my head. Turns out some peacocks have escaped from Prospect Park Zoo, and the ass rush is on to find them before they are roadkill on Flatbush Avenue. Don't think about Moxie pancaked on asphalt. No one's seen my snow-white pirate-eyed dog.

A mother-daughter duo, carbon copies down to their pink candle lips, picnic in the vanilla air. The mother has the kind of obscene beauty that makes you ache just to see it. The daughter hasn't grown into hers, yet. The way you look. If she's not careful, that chorus will score her life:

I'll manage the money; you smile for the camera. The way you look...

What do you mean "no"? The way you look. You're practically begging me for it.

The way you look? You wouldn't understand.

Jesus mother fucking Christ, I want to drown in a bathtub of Black Label, but no such goddamn luck. Search for mercy in the woodlands of the park's ravine. A light breeze tickles the leaves skyward. Small streams spool among tree trunks, tinkling like ice cubes as they cascade over rocks. In the aging day, something alabaster plays tag with the shrubs.

'Moxie?' As I run, my ankles bend at odd angles like the old trees surrounding me. Whatever it is, it's fucking fast! Shit-cock! I've lost it. Behind me, something gossamer is airborne. A perfectly white peacock lands a few feet away and fans its opalescent fringe. He wears his plumage like a wedding dress, his train of feathers all confetti and lace. A calmness akin to grace drapes over me. It's that moment when one thing allows itself into another. The bird turns his head an impossible angle and regards me with a take it or leave it quality. I bend down so we are level. He curves his head inward, nestling it under his own wing, inhaling his own private smell. His feathers feel like filigreed cotton candy. A moment of wordless pleasure. He unfurls his neck into a languid S and pins me with his pondwater-colored eye before disappearing into the purpling evening.

✳

I awake to an acid-blue sky. Not even nine, and it's as hot as fuck. There's a missed call from my ex-agent Estelle. She repped me after Mom did, after that first summer in Paris, during the in-between. Haven't heard from her since my meteoric ascent. Seems she's submitted me for a go-see at two, clean-clean. It's lingerie catalogue work, not 'the Victoria's Secret Fashion Shows you're accustomed to' and reminds me that beggars can't be choosers.

"Clean-clean" means no makeup, no body hair. Naked as a snowman, I stand in front of my full-length mirror. A slight alcohol bloat threatens my belly. Fuckety-fuck Estelle, a little notice would have been nice. Submitting me must have been an afterthought. I've never had to do catalogue work, not even when I was starting out, thanks to that Pirelli calendar.

Despite the heat, I put on some heavy sweats and a hoodie and head north along Kent. The East River is strafed with light. Run until I'm raining. Sweat rushes over my singed skin, burning and itching. I want to rake my face. Tap my nails against my cheek instead of clawing it. Pinpricks of hot/cold pain numb my cheekbone. I run faster, crossing the invisible line between safety and danger. The river glisters. Tap my nails harder, triggering a fire burst on my skin. I want to rip it off. One nail scrapes. I cry out. They say grief is pain trying to flee the body. I sprint. I grate. Tears outrun my chin.

✱

The go-see is a cattle call. Herds of women who never made it to the top grapple for a toehold on their skid to the bottom. Stand in the corner, right side facing the wall, portfolio at my feet. It's been years since I had to carry it.

'Excuse me,' the voice comes from a sinewy yoga body. 'Could you sign this?' She thrusts forward an open issue of Elle. My before-face stares out from a John Hardy ad. Peel myself off the wall to sign it. A roomful of iPhones captures the moment. I can see the Twitter feed: Beauty is Beast.

'Thanks. I'm a huge fan. You're #MyCalvins ad made me want to model.'

My smile is a nose wrinkle.

'You looked so powerful. In your eyes. Like you knew things.'

'Most people who saw that ad probably didn't notice my eyes.' Should have called it #MyAss.

'Well, like yeah, obviously, it was about your body. But it was more than that too. Can I ask you something?'

Either the room is shrinking or everybody has taken a step closer. God of shit. Is that woman with the soap opera hair filming?

'What does it feel like?'

'Total abandon, if you surrender to it. Modeling is adult make-believe, with better sets and costumes.'

'Not that. This.' She touches her right cheek. 'To go from John Hardy to this.'

The coming years unfold before me. It's like an orgasm, but bad. Thousands of invisible needles jolt me with feelings. Also like an orgasm, it's brief. Outside, an ambulance siren stops mid-sentence. 'Disbelief.' A single word satisfies the complicated question of my life.

'I'm sure it will get better.' She smiles the vacant smile of vegans.

'And I'm sure you'll have a big career.'

'Wow. Thanks. That means a lot coming from you.'

She doesn't know that false hope hurts like a broken heart.

'Number 78, they're ready for you.' The casting assistant's voice is a friendless harmonica. Grab my portfolio and follow it.

"How are you today?' the assistant asks politely, not wanting an answer. Her face is full of unhelpful Botox. She leads me into an inner office and closes the door as she exits. A doughy middle-aged white guy comes out from behind a desk. He should be managing a used Chevy dealership.

'Hello, Jax. I'm Marty. Estelle and I go way back.'

Marty's handshake exceeds the recommended time limit.

'She explained your situation. Maybe we can help each other out.'

Light reflects off the oily horseshoe ring of hair outlining Marty's bald head as he pages through my book.

'It's not editorial. Straight up catalogue work. No glamour shots. No face.' He appraises me from neck to knees. 'I think you could work. You know the drill. Go behind that curtain and change into the swimsuit. We'll take some pictures and see.'

How many women have tried this shit on?

'Let's get some walking shots.'

I step forward with my front leg nice and long, front arm extended back, opposite arm long and forward, my head at three quarters. Step back, looking at my imaginary friends, and forth about one hundred times as Marty works his camera. Used to do this in eight-inch needle heels.

'Great. Let's get some stills. Front. Nice. Now back. Perfect. Profile, and half turn. Ok, we're done. You can change.'

When I return, Marty's poured some wine.

'Here's to new beginnings.'

The wine tastes like a saddle.

'And to seeing more of you, Jax.'

You've just taken pictures of me in a bikini. What's there left to see? Drain my glass. 'You'll see me when you call me in for castings.'

'Yeah?' He looks like a dog waiting to be fed.

'Yeah. No braid of legs.'

'There's more to me than meets the eye.'

'I know.' He's an original stereotype.

'You should know,' he looks directly at the ruins of my face. 'Especially now.' He takes my empty glass. 'And lay off the booze. It's starting to affect your figure.'

Heat melts the asphalt on Broadway as I head toward Union Square. Mother-ass mother fucker! Like I'd do-si-do for fucking catalogue work. Is this what my career has come to? I hurl my portfolio down, the front and back covers spreading apart on the sidewalk. Bet Marty has sludgy sex, when he can find his chimpy shrimp dick below his Pillsbury belly. And I should lay off the booze? Fuck you Marty! And fuck you Estelle. You're as bad as Mom. Might as well take it to the streets if I'm going to be pimped. The only difference is location. Bend down to retrieve my portfolio and everything spills out. There are tear sheets from Burberry, Gucci and Chanel; Sports Illustrated Swimsuit Issue and #MyCalvins stills. That Victoria's Secret Holiday ad. Professional constructions of physical perfection. Look south on Broadway to where it crosses Fifth at Madison Square, the building-lined streets forming the "V" of an open zipper. What has happened and what will happen erase themselves at the apex of the Flatiron Building. Hold up the #MyCalvins ad. Yoga Body Girl was right: there is something in the eyes. Poke my fingernails through them. Rip my face out of the picture. Ripping the first makes ripping the others easier. I litter the ground. Last is the Pirelli calendar.

'Wait. I'll give you two hundred for it.' A pair of Prada loafers as molten as *pot de créme* strides into view.

Fuck that. The calendar is coveted because you can't buy it and because it shows the world's most beautiful women in various degrees of undress. City sounds fill the space between us.

'Three.' His metrosexual voice tightens.

'A grand.' Turn my head and look directly at him. His face is a viola.

His eyes bounce off my charred cheek but return. They darken as they hold my gaze. 'Five.'

'Bruce Weber shot it.' Stand up to show him the calendar. 'Sienna Miller, Isabeli Fontana, Heidi Klum, Sophie Dahl.'

'Is that you?' He takes the calendar, re-registering me. The carnal bloom of my teenage self stares back at us.

'A lifetime ago.'

He looks down at where we're standing. Pieces of me are stuck to the bottoms of his shoes. 'You've had quite a career.'

Had. Past tense.

'Keep it.' He hands the calendar back. 'You'll want it someday.'

My wanting is a wilderness.

Halfway down the block, he stops to scrape his heels against the pavement.

(Did she take the calendar and portfolio case to the nearest bar and barter them for drinks? Did she stumble like a drunk mule and then pass out just beyond the steps of the Bedford Avenue L stop in the shadow of a taco truck? Did a friend find her among a herd of Manhattan tourists snapping pictures of supermodel road kill for Instagram and Twitter? It's so real it looks fake. Did you retweet?)

✱

I wake somewhere between drunkenness and consequence. My forehead flares blue/red. At least the pillow beside me is empty: no lying dismantled by a mistake. Through a sea of sound that makes no sense comes Frieda carrying a glass of-. When did I get a blender?

Frieda opens the blinds. The sky is ruffled. 'She lives.'

So to speak.

'Here.' She hands me a glass of pea-green liquid. 'Drink this.'

My mouth already tastes like a dying rat crapped in it.

'I'm telling, not asking.' She sits on the edge of my bed. Her sobriety is unsettling. I take a few sips while we have a not-conversation. 'What happened?'

'I was hoping you could tell me.' I cough. This green shit is chunky. It paces my esophagus.

Frieda's face twists into something I don't recognize. 'If you check Instagram and Twitter, you'll know what I know. What happened before?' She hands me my phone.

Jesus mother fucking Christ...Fuck. Fuck. Fuck! And fuck some more. A public pictorial of my bottoming out is garnishing Instagram followers faster than a Kardashian crisis. Some art director wannabe fuck placed a burrito next to my passed-out open mouth, creamy white sauce dripping down the burrito's side like it had already blown its load. A Twitter feed includes links to photos from the autograph session in the waiting room of the lingerie go-see. Yoga Body Girl has left an aphoristic message.

'I had a go-see.'

'Then what? I found you ass out on Bedford.'

My brain goes on a walkabout. Images slip through my fingers until a cold clarity crystallizes inside the haze. 'Did I have my portfolio?'

'You had shit girl. I had to fish your key out of your pocket.'

I feel like I'm being suspended in a vast wind tunnel.

'Jax,' Frieda's voice is freeze dried. 'You have a problem.'

'Just one?'

'You drink too much. You need some help.'

'No I don't.'

Frieda's face is inches from mine. 'Girl, take a good long look at reality. Your career is over, but your life isn't. Stop drinking it away.'

We enter a staring contest moment, with me quietly can't standing her.

'Right. I'll give you some time to think.' Frieda stands. 'Where's your ball-loving beast? She probably needs a walk.'

'I can barely take care of myself.' Mutter her words at her. Stand up and weave my way to the kitchen as a tiny garden gnome with a big stick beats out a steady rhythm above my eyebrows.

'What was that?' Frieda's on my heels.

'You were right. I can't take care of myself, much less a dog. Lost her in Prospect Park. Was– Where's my Johnnie Walker?' Our eyes skid into each other.

'I dumped it.'

'Fuck you Frieda.' My nostrils flair with impotent rage. 'You had no right to do that.'

'You were passed out in a gutter.'

'So fucking what. Like you've never over-indulged.' I hide behind a shield of righteousness. Pick up Moxie's crusted food bowl and wash it as if doing some housework will make the real problems disappear. 'Was walking Moxie with that stoner from Teddy's and then she was gone. He said he'd put up some flyers.'

'Jax-'

'I don't have any pictures of her anyway.'

'So go to the shelter where you got her and see if they have one. Stop waiting for someone else to save you.'

'I'm not waiting for someone to save me.' Hurl Moxie's bowl to the ground. 'Don't you fucking touch me.'

'You're at war with yourself, not with me.'

'The fuck I am.' The room fills with mad girl breath. The dark part of me aches.

'What happened in Marrakesh wasn't your fault. You can't let it determine you.'

'Nothing will ever change this.' Scrape my face and relish the pain rush.

'Stop it.' Frieda quickly overpowers me. 'You will never look like you used to. You need to accept that.'

'You're so full of shit.' Beneath Frieda's glitz, I see a little boy wanting to be a girl.

'What is that supposed to mean?' Frieda's face transforms into a familiar stranger's.

'I don't see you dressing like a man.'

Her slap is fast but restrained.

Cruelty is a poor defense against sadness.

✳

When I wake, dusk has shifted to stars. The skin crawl of being alone pushes me from my apartment to Alat's where the beer garden is packed. A round of applause greets me at the entrance, thieving me of my anonymity. Eye shush it and head inside to sit on the other side of attention.

'Kaifik habibi?' Alat wears a poker face.

'Cackling at life. Kaifa?'

'Hamdullah.'

'The usual, please.' There are five missed calls from a number I don't recognize. Scroll through my Facebook feed and then stop cold. Something inside me screws tighter. There's a picture of Coke Nose from an old Zara ad with a RIP caption. Step off what I know before I know. Click over to her page to find hundreds of pop song tributes praising her outer and inner beauty. Death encourages BFF marketing: anyone who can, lays claim, posting personal photos and group selfies.

'Do you know about this?' Show Alat my phone.

'Heard about it yesterday. Accidental overdose.'

From the glass, Johnnie Walker watches me. 'Her poor family,' because that's the type of shit you're supposed to say.

'A waste of a life.' Alat's comment is freighted with meaning. It pokes me from across a bridge of sighs. 'You get only one, Jax.'

The phone in my hand rings. 'Sorry, I need to take this.' Turn away from the bar with Alat's eyes in my back. 'Hello?'

'Miss Jax, you're hard to reach.'

'How did you get my number?'

'I can't reveal my source, but let's just say he has some killer photos.'

'That's not funny. I thought you were better than that. I'm hanging up.'

'What? Wait Jax. It's Lukas.'

'I know who this is. I just didn't think you were the type to kick a girl when she's down.' Right now, I wish I could put my forehead on Moxie's forehead.

'I'm not. What are you talking about?'

'The killer photos.'

'What about them? Dylan shot some great candids of you in the loft the other day. I understand why you were a supermodel.'

Were. My mouth twists into an ugly "S". 'That's The Dylan.'

'Do you call him that?'

'I can't call him that.'

'What did you think I was talking about?'

'Forget it. So, to what do I owe the pleasure?'

'I want to write about you for The New Yorker. Thanks to The Dylan's pictures, I've got a green light from the features editor.'

'You can drop the "The".'

'Is that a yes?'

'No.'

'What would it take to convince you?'

Curing me of myself. 'What've you got?'

'Once people read it, who knows what could happen.'

'Yeah, what could happen for you.' Blow off a layer to hear beneath the bullshit.

'No, for you. You shouldn't be a coffee gopher. Telling your story is a step forward.'

'What if I don't want my story told.' How do you fold down a life?

'I'm looking at Twitter now. You're story's being told whether you want it to be or not. This way, at least you frame the narrative.'

'You sound like the White House press secretary.'

'You never fail to surprise me. Jax, I hear the story hiding inside your voice. Let's tell it.'

'What would I have to do?'

'Why don't we meet and I can outline my ideas. If you like them, we'll hang out a few times and talk.'

I'm not sure I want to enter Lukas's city of questions. 'This is not a yes.'

'Do you have time tomorrow?'

'I'm busy,' I lie. 'How about the day after?'

'Sounds good. Do you know The Half King on West Twenty-Third? Let's meet at 2.'

'See you then.' As I hang up, a Mexican delivery boy plops a paper bag on the bar in front of me. 'I didn't order that.'

The delivery boy stares at me as if I were a car crash. 'It's from that table outside.' He points at a cock-fuck sampling of post-college frat boys raising their beer mugs to me. They look like they've been vended by Mattel for eight bucks a pop. Inside the bag a burrito dribbles sour cream.

Slip a ten in the delivery boy's hand as I give him back the bag. 'See that guy with the Don Draper hair?' Point to a frat Twinkie smiling with coital suggestiveness. 'Bring it to him and tell him I'm not hungry for what he's got.' When he gets the burrito back, Frat Twinkie jumps on the table and humps the air in my direction. Is he sexy or alarming?

Googling Lukas is a welcomed distraction. His writing is like brain sex: intimate, generous, feeling. Reading it lets me rummage around in the cupboards of his mind and leaves me roiling, restless. Is there some secret drawer where we can lie like spoons? In his Rikers piece, Lukas profiles a kid who was sent there because someone said he stole a backpack. He couldn't pay his bail, so he sat in Rikers, waiting for his trial. The kid lost almost three years, a lot of it in solitary, without ever being tried or convicted. When the kid says, "There are certain things that changed about me and they might not go back," I shiver like water in the wind.

'Since you didn't like the burrito, can I buy you a drink?' Frat Twinkie must have come inside to use the bathroom. He gives off a testicular air.

'Black Label, straight up. Water back. Nice Magic Mike moves.' If you like foreplay aerobics.

'We all have our talents.' He crosses to my left side. 'My name's Brian.'

'Jax.' Alat brings a fresh round. 'Your fly is open. Cheers.'

Brian hiccups on his shot then assumes a posture of masculine nonchalance. I watch him zip up with my measuring tape eyes. His build suggests good old grass-fed Americana. In the beer garden, his crew is clearing out.

'Do you like what you see?' Brian's laugh is like loose change rattling around the bottom of a paper cup.

'Some.'

'I'm not used to such frank scrutiny.'

'I am.' The way you look. 'How does it feel?'

'From you? Flattering. From the bartender? Probably not as good.'

'Let me do it again.' My stare pushes his legs ever so slightly apart.

'My turn.'

Hold my profile position. 'I'm not done looking.'

'Afraid to face me?'

'No.'

'Then look at me woman.' He unbuttons restraint.

Turn my head and lower my eyes, imagining the taut plain of pelvis, his smooth, stiff shaft. I'm ready for some loveless fucking.

'Look me in the eye.'

I level my stare. Watch the light in his eyes dim as he takes in my physical ruin and brighten again as he leaves it. I lay my hand over my heart as his eyes transverse my breasts. My hand accompanies his gaze as it caresses my thigh. When his eyes return to my face, they nest in my lips. It feels like a kiss. I am plugged in.

'Good God, woman.'

'No one calls me that.'

'What?'

'Woman. Usually it's "girl".'

'Trust me. You're all woman.'

'You ready to go?'

'Where?'

'Your place.' I want to wild out.

'See? Woman.' Brian finishes my water. 'What if I'm not that type of guy?'

'I will be greatly disappointed.'

'What about your place?'

'My husband's home.' Why not make a game of life?

'I hope you're kidding.'

'Would it matter?' Slather a look of concern across my face.

'It might. Depends on how many friends he has.'

'He's a loner. That's why he's home.'

Outside there are more stars than we need.

'This way.' Brian heads toward the East River and the condominium towers where money lives. We pause near the ferry dock to watch moonlight play hide and seek with the waves. Turn to him and feather my lips along the lush cup of his mouth. Kiss him in time to the secret breathing of the pier. His lips taste mysteriously of figs. What does he taste in me?

'Let's go.' Brian voice is a speed bump in the silence. As we enter the building, he nods at the doorman who gives me a tough, slithered look. Hey buddy, you can't tickle yourself.

Our conversation takes on a shapeless quality until we are lying naked, my tongue graffitiing his body. The ridges of his ribs morph into river waves, his cock becomes the North Fifth Street Pier, his keen loan moan echoes the foghorns haunting the East River. I put him inside me and ride him to the rhythm of Merengue blasting from the Puerto Rican bodegas east of the Brooklyn-Queens Expressway. Outside his bedroom window, darkness stands back behind the persevering skyline. In my mind's eye, the industrial warehouses glow under a slow sun. I come, triggering an internal sunburst. Brian comes, his eyes all dark and buttony with pleasure. Unsticking skin from skin, I roll off him into an airy, bottomless quiet. We lie coated in the starch of sex.

He looks happy but with something else on his face too.

The air between us changes.

He watches me cover my body with clothes again. 'You don't have to go.'

'I know,' and finish dressing.

'At least let me take you.'

Brian probably walks curbside while escorting the ladies and gets all the doors. 'That's OK.' My words reflect on his face. Outside, the predawn light is a translucent, misty blue. I want to live in the all of it.

'Why so cold? I thought we had a good time.'

'We did. But now we're done.' I can't help he's fucked my attraction to him right out of me. Find my left shoe under a chair. Replace the door as I leave.

PART THREE

The sky is shut under a grey lid of clouds as I make my way to the animal shelter on Bedford. The woman behind the counter is dabbling with being young again—she keeps hiking up the waist band on her skinny jeans to cover the whale tail of her thong. Lean on the counter with my best face forward and wait for her to notice me above the wild racket.

When she sees me, her mouth forms an open change purse. 'How can I help you?'

She looks like somebody who tries to try. 'I got a dog here last week,' pause to thrust some papers forward, 'and I was wondering if you have any photos of her.'

'Why don't you just snap one with your iPhone?' Her noodle arms fold across her chest in self-congratulations.

'Excuse me,' I whisper as if we're part of a sisterhood. 'Do you know your thong is showing?'

Tug. Tug. Her manicure is self-inflicted.

'Maybe you could look in your records?' Point to a reference number on my receipt. She looks calm and flustered all at once. 'It would mean a lot.' Will some tears. Bless my ability to appear desperate with dignity.

'Well, just this once. I'll need to check on the computer in back. Don't take anything.' My receipt leaves with her.

I'm disfigured, not criminal. 'Of course not.' My need masks my rage as I watch her walk away.

Tug. I find Moxie.

Tug. I find Moxie not.

Tug. I find Moxie.

She disappears inside some inner sanctum and returns moments later holding a printout. Was that so hard?

She turns to me with a pleasant, pointed look. 'What do you need this for again?' and holds fast to the photo.

A film of dust coats the counter. I draw Snoopy in it. 'I need to make a missing dog flyer.'

'You lost your dog after only a week?' she snaps her tongue.

Did all the animals just quiet down?

'I didn't lose her. She ran away in the park.'

'You *lost* her.' Her lips compress into a line. I see her twentysomething self, counting up a lifetime of dollars saved from drunk uncles before her move to the big city.

'Fine, I lost her.' Sometimes you have to go along to get along.

'I don't suppose you had gotten her an ID tag or a microchip?'

'No.'

'In a week? You don't deserve her.'

I hold my anger close to me like a baby.

Her face puffs with generosity. 'I'm giving you this for the sake of the dog. Not everyone is qualified to have a pet.'

Take the photo and give her a bright, furious smile. 'Or to wear skinny jeans.' Turn on my heels and strut out. Fuck! There was a time when people used to fall over themselves doing things for me they shouldn't. Now they don't want to do the things they should.

✸

The day has a washed out feeling. I stop at Internet Garage to scan Moxie's photo and print some flyers, and then catch the Q train to Prospect Park to put them up. Surface at Parkside Avenue and don't know where to start. Moxie could have gone in any direction whereas there are several neighborhood bars right in front of me. Shitty fuck. I forgot tape. This is hopeless. Am heading toward Delroy's Café when the memory of Moxie running her crazy dog circles rushes me. Cross the street and enter Duane Reade instead. Wander the aisles in search of something adhesive. Pass bags of Milky Ways and stacks of jumbo-sized Kit Kats before stopping in front of a pyramid of Toblerones. The triangular prism of chocolate is weighty in the palm of my hand. My mouth waters with the memory of sugary, milky cocoa butter giving way to nougat, almonds and honey. Replace the Toblerone and am pointing at some Reese's Minis when I feel the telltale warmth of a person next to me.

'Do they respond?' A familiar, creamy voice drips into my right ear and leaks down my neck.

'Yes. They share the secrets of a parallel universe.' At least the rising blush doesn't show on my charred cheek. 'What are you doing here?'

'I live over here, remember?' Today's Richard's eyes are the color of wine bottles. 'What are you doing here?'

'I'm getting tape to put these up.' Pull a flyer from the paper bag inside my purse.

'So you haven't found her?'

Shake my head. 'Didn't you offer to help?'

'That I did.'

'Still up for it?'

'Sure. Tape is this way.'

Back outside, the air is thick with the promise of rain. Sweat shellacs the stubble above Richard's upper lip as he ponytails his hair into a pine cone. 'Where do you want to start?'

'I have no idea.' Oh how I miss the days of a fashion editor telling me what to do.

'This way.' He crosses Flatbush Avenue into the heart of Prospect Leffert Gardens with me shadowing his heroin chic frame. We plaster Moxie's photo in storefront windows, on traffic light poles and at subway entrances. Halfway through the neighborhood, the clouds erupt into a theatrical rain. Running through the streets feels like surfing a grey wave. Richard grabs my hand and shortcuts toward his apartment building. Rain blows in, sparking the linoleum. We trail water through the hallway to his front door. 'Come on in.' Dean is waiting for Richard on the other side of the threshold.

'Thanks.' Inside, I slip off my sandals and drip onto a small, hand-woven rug.

'You can come all the way in.' Richard bows his head to ruffle Dean's neck. A few drops of water roll off his scalp and soak into Dean's fur.

'How's his eye?' I pet Dean, whose snout is a compass needle for Richard.

'About the same.' Richard removes his soaked tee. His chest is smooth and tan while his back is inked with tribal designs. He opens a closet and hands me a towel. 'Here.'

'Thanks.'

'Do you want some dry clothes?'

'That'd be great.' Outside the window, tree leaves glitter and yawn.

Richard disappears into a back room and returns with some sweat pants and a t-shirt. 'The bathroom's the door on the left.'

Doesn't he know that models are used to changing their clothes in front of anyone? Ex-model. Inside the bathroom, there's a box of Preference by L'Oréal peeking out from behind the shower curtain. By the time I've changed, Richard's splayed on his sofa, lighting a joint. 'You smoke?' He slides over to make room for me.

Why not? The cherry burns a brighter red. Lay my head back and feel it helicopter away. My eyes gain weight. Under my eyelids, red and blue pinpoints bubble upwards.

'You okay?' Richard's voice come to me across a canyon.

My lips refuse to shape sound. They flatten into a half-smile. 'Kayh.'

I can't react to his laughter.

'Take it easy.' He rescues the blunt from my fingertips as his head docks in my lap, his neck resting on the hill of my hip.

'Make ysel comf ta pul.' Richard's hair begs to be freed. I pet it. We drift in silence.

Rolling halfway off the couch wakes me. Cock one eye open to see Richard splitting an avocado. Darkness cleaves to the kitchen window as I ravel myself back to being. 'What time is it?'

'About nine. You hungry?' He slaps two steaks into a frying pan.

'Some.' My body is stiff with couch sleep. Realize that Richard is watching me stretch. Arch my back to give him a better view. 'Need some help?'

'Sure.'

Shit. Was counting on his saying no so we might fuck around. 'What can I do?'

'You can slice the rest of those avocados.'

Great. The knife is awkward in my grip.

'Like this.' He snaps the rubber band on my wrist before his hand guides my hand. My face gets hot.

'Thanks. I don't cook.'

'No kidding.' He flips the steaks.

'I mean, I don't know how to cook.'

'No kidding.' He takes my primitive avocado pieces and dresses them in lime juice, salt and pepper. Adds some fresh basil from a window sill plant. 'What were you dreaming about?'

'When?'

'On the sofa.'

For a second, I am seven years old, watching a bedroom door as if I could make it open. The memory shreds and fades. 'I don't remember.'

'You were making some kooky sounds.'

'Like what?'

Richard plates the steaks. 'You were making sounds like a bee. BZZZZZ. You know?'

'Crazy. How much salad do you want?' Avocado jags slither off a wooden serving spoon onto our plates. 'This kitchen's pretty well set-up.'

'You sound surprised. Not everyone lives off take-out.' Richard grabs two beers from his refrigerator.

'You mean room service.' I follow him with our plates to the table. 'I'm kidding.' Not really.

Dean rises from his dog bed to snuggle by Richard's chair. 'If it's stopped raining, I should take him for a walk.'

'OK. We could check on how many missing Moxie flyers are still hanging.'

Richard serves me a look.

'My bad. You didn't invite me to join you.'

'It's all good. You could post Moxie's picture on your Facebook or Instagram.'

'I already have.' The piece of meat I'm chewing grows bigger inside my mouth. Fork the rest of my steak onto Richard's plate.

'Don't you like it?'

'It's great. I'm not that hungry.'

'Right.' Richard rolls another joint. 'So, what do you do all day?'

'Nothing.'

'Must be nice.'

'It's not.' To be loose in the world.

'What do you want to do?'

'Model. What do you want to do?'

'I'm waiting for pot to become legal and then I want to grow it.'

That explains the copy of *The Cannabis Grow Bible* among the DVDs on his bookshelf. It's the only book in sight. Stand up and carry my plate to the sink. 'The rain's stopped.' Outside the window, a few stars dot the night sky. 'Want to go?'

'In a minute.' Richard lights up. 'Why do you want to model?'

How do you explain living at the center of the center? That every shoot is a fresh take? 'It's the only thing I've ever wanted to do.'

'That's not a reason.'

'It's the only thing I know how to do.' Sometimes I think I should have finished high school.

'It seems dumb.'

'It's not. If you're good, there's this moment of connection with the camera, and if the photographer's good, he catches it. That moment is ...' An untellable rush. How did my hands get on his shoulders?

'Jax, what're you doing?'

Speaking complicates the air.

'I think I'm making a move.' Breathe my words along his neck, into his ear. My lips arrange themselves along his neck slowly, asking permission.

Richard's hands cupping my ass and lifting me into a straddle across his lap seems like a yes. My fingers twine into his hair. Kiss down his smooth chest to his flat stomach and rub my tits over his dick. Use my tongue to open his body. Slither my way up and open my eyes to watch us kissing. He opens his eyes too. They hook onto my scabs. Incredibly close and face to face, something in his irises blears. He squeezes his eyes under their lids. His supple lips tighten. 'Jax.' He takes his fingers out of me. 'Wait.' Wipes them on my hip as he lifts me off of him, leaving a smeary print. 'Stop.' He removes my hand from his cock; unrealized potential. 'I can't.'

I take a moment to stall. 'What's wrong?'

'I can't.'

'Turn me around.'

A moment of soul silence in which I'm stripped of all fuck value.

'No.' He rests his hand between my shoulder blades and adds some rewarmed words. 'I'm sorry.'

I feel like a pretend woman.

Fuck. Why can't he be a fuck-crazy asshole? Should have waited for him to finish the blunt. My fingers trace the left side of my face. It's calming to touch my beauty and know some of it is still there. 'I should go.'

'You don't have to run off.'

My vision of us lying naked and satiated stutters. 'That's okay.' Throw off his clothes while I look for my own. Let him see what he's missing.

Richard's eyes follow my reverse strip tease. 'Are you okay?'

'Why wouldn't I be?' Conjure myself from clothing.

'Okay.'

'You're the one who'll be kicking yourself. You could have had a supermodel. Think of the stories.' My voice is something I can't quite catch and hold on to. Exit into the cobalt part of night.

I am in this alone.

A man with strong breath and bags under his eyes solicits outside the Sterling Street subway entrance. He wears a thick layer of city. Drop some coins in his cup before clearing the turn style. The smell of alcohol mixes with vomit and piss—the witches' brew of the underground. A few people crabwalk along the 2, 5 platform. Sitting alone on a bench, a woman hugs a Michael Kors handbag to her chest, her mouth slackening a little, foreshadowing the coming years which will ossify her face. On some other day, on some other platform, she could be my mother.

The train rumbles into the barrel of the station. Inside, the car smells of Fritos and wet socks. A Chaplinesque man totters down the aisle and falls into a seat as the train lurches forward. Farther down, a group of millennials marvel at the popularity of Trump, that short-fingered vulgarian.

'You sure are ugly.' The voice trumpets from a young brown face haloed by dandelion seeds of hair.

'Only half. See?'

'Wow.' He claps his hands and laughs at my magic trick. 'Do it again.'

Wag my head from side to side.

'Does it hurt?'

'Sometimes.'

A done-in voice calls from the far end of the car. 'Terek, don't be bothering strangers.' Terek's head bobbles on his neck toward a stormy-faced woman holding a Sponge Bob balloon and a stuffed orange tiger.

'I ain't bothering her.' Terek yells down the aisle like it's his living room. 'She's lonely.' Laughter wiggles out of motionless faces. Terek hops onto the seat next to me. 'Want one?' He holds open a Mickey D's bag where French fries jelly together.

'No thanks.'

'Why not? They're good.' He licks his fingers and then stuffs some fries inside his mouth. 'How'd you get a face like that?' The fries match the color of his teeth.

'An accident.' My single story.

'She had an accident.' Terek yells to the car in general. Faces swivel in our direction, forming a homely quilt of mismatched expressions. 'She okay now.' Terek prances on the seats back to his mother. There's something in the curve of her back that makes her heavy. Terek whispers in her ear and she hands him the balloon. He gallops back to me.

'Here.' Terek holds out the balloon string, a thumb newly moved into his mouth.

'I can't take your Sponge Bob.'

'I don't like him.' He ties the string into a bow around my wrist.

'Thank you.' Should I give him some money? Standing, 'I change trains here. Bye Terek.'

'Bye half-pretty lady.'

Stand in front of the sliding glass doors, my fractured face caught in the roaring darkness of the tunnel. I stare at my reflection: an end and a beginning collide at the seam of the doors.

✳

Lay in bed open-eyed and blind in the dark. Curl onto my side and I am five years old, wrapped around my Raggedy Ann doll with her Band-Aided foot inside my mouth. From the kitchen come angry voices, all gross and foreign. The history between those voices hardens, breaks. Roll onto my stomach and I'm eight or nine. Mom and I are lying side by side on the Jersey Shore, the day's sun pinking our noses. I chatter about snow cones and lightning bugs and Hello Kitty stickers because preventing silence is a full-time job. Flip onto my back and I am twelve. Hold hands with myself in my lap as 'Uncle Rodney" creeps his palm onto my knee and Mom pretends not to see.

Snap. The sting from the rubber band catapults me from bed. Pull open the closet door and snatch a box filled with emotional scree. Memories flit in and out of focus. I yank journals from the box, ripping their pages free, flaking the bedroom floor with confetti teeth. Crumple paper into paper and create a giant collaged ball. Favela music rushes through my window from some passing car. I rut through the closet for any remaining tear sheets and pile them onto a stack tipsy with photographs. Cart the whole of it to a dumpster as the sun pulls pink streamers across the sky. Down the street, a girl exits a taxi, her hair billowing into a banner behind her.

✳

Light froths the room as minutes catch up and collect. Share blue morning time with Johnny Walker before heading to Prospect Park South to resume the search for Moxie. Waste an hour wandering the loudly quiet Historic

District where people don't seem to live. The mansions are as still as the relentlessly dark apartments that rim Central Park. Veer west through neighborhood row houses fighting an architectural class war into Windsor Terrace. Post a flyer outside the Food Co-op before pausing at the Brooklyn Public Library to hang Moxie's photo next to a sign advertising free computer classes. Farther down Fort Hamilton Parkway, four socked-and-sandaled retirees throw bocce balls on the asphalt adjacent to the Immaculate Heart of Mary. They needle one another in a mixture of Italian and English. Off to the side, a Regina's Bakery box sags with cannoli, surrounded by drained paper coffee cups.

Red brick row houses flying the American flag stand sentry along Seeley Street. A shiny black Prius rolls up to a bay-windowed fortress and parks under a London plane tree. A colt of a girl exits from the back seat and prances up the front steps to wait in the cool of the porch. The driver, a high-school band-leader type, crosses to the passenger side and scoops a white bundle into his arms. 'Here we go. Nice and easy.' He holds it like a baby. He leans his face forward for a nose licking. The bundle emits a shallow teakettle bark.

Rush forward and trip over a section of tree root dislodging the sidewalk. Is my heart visibly beating? 'Excuse me,' I call as he opens his front door.

As he turns, the bundle trains its pirate-eyed face in my direction. Its right hind leg is bandaged.

'Moxie?' The bundle barks.

The man's eyes tick tock between my face and the girl's. He shoes her into the house, slamming the door shut behind them.

Rush the front door and lay on bell. No answer. The curtains in the bay window rustle back into place. Ring the bell in time to the slow scream inside my head.

An upstairs window opens. 'If you don't leave, I'm calling the police.'

My voice goes swarmy. 'I just want to ask you about your dog.'

'You've got until the count of three to vacate my property.' The man's voice holds a taint of junior high bullying: stolen lunch money, being trapped inside a gym locker, pushed on stairs.

'Please. Just come to the door.'

'One—'

'My dog ran away and—'

'Two—' he pushes on the word like it's the last bit of Crest at the bottom of the tube.

'Okay, Okay. I'm going.' Take a missing dog flyer from my bag and shove it under his "Welcome!" mat, the sad irony of the thing. Is it brave or weak to leave someone behind?

✳

Propelled by will and not instinct, I head to The Half King in neutral daylight. The bar area is droozy with late lunch sangria drinkers. A quiet room off to the right is where I find Lukas studying a photography exhibit about undocumented immigrants travelling from Central America to the US/Mexico border. Most of the subjects are young men and women carrying children, or are children themselves, tethered atop a freight train, embarking on an odyssey across a belligerent wasteland.

'Glad you could make it.' That handshake again, that rutted road voice. Lukas guides us to a table beneath a photograph of a Salvadorian migrant breast-feeding her son on the bare floor of a Catholic shelter.

'No problem.'

Lukas slicks down his cowlick, which immediately springs upright. I bet his parents took hundreds of pictures of it when he was a baby.

'How've you been?' He looks at me with concern in one eye and skepticism in the other.

'Rollicking. You?'

'Good. Busy. Criminal justice system reform is having its moment in the spotlight.'

'I read your Rikers piece. Congratulations.'

'Thanks.' His recently shaved neck is tall and shy. 'Have you eaten here before? The burgers are pretty good.'

'Can I start you guys out with something to drink?' The waitress shakes her hair so it swings out in a skirt. When she turns in my direction, her face is an egg.

'Black Label straight up, Brooklyn Lager back.' I'm not so much hungry as empty.

Lukas hesitates and shuts his menu. 'Make it two.'

'Two Brooklyn Lagers and two shots of Black. Are you ready to order or do you need a few minutes?' She looks at Lukas, drinking him in. At me, she takes small glances like sips.

'Jax?'

'I'm good.' Hold my menu up to the waitress.

'Are you sure? Okay. I'll have a burger, medium rare. Thanks.' He hands the waitress our menus and watches her sash away, his eyes sheepish and wolfish at the same time. He probably fucks with a balance between hostility and tenderness. 'How are you?'

Didn't we just do that? I smile like the hostess of a party she regrets having.

'I'm worried about you.'

I finger a rogue period hair beneath my chin. 'You don't know me enough to be worried about me.'

'What happened the other day?'

How about waiting for the alcohol softener? 'Why do you care?'

'Maybe I can help.'

Lukas's eyes glide over the room before his hand slicks to my side of the table to pluck at my rubber band. His fingernails shine. 'This is the part where you say something.'

'Because of some shady flirtation?' Pull my hand away.

'Because it helps.'

'I thought you were supposed to be talking. Outlining your ideas and convincing me to be interviewed.'

'Here we are. Two Black Labels, two Brooklyns. Your burger will be out shortly.' The waitress tucks her hair behind her ear like a comma. Her cheek looks unwholesomely tender in the dubious bar light.

Reach for my shot. Hello Lovely!

'Wait.' Lukas holds his shot before him.

'What?' The glass is halfway to my mouth.

'We have to toast.'

Tink the bottom of my glass into his and make lip contact with the rim before he stops me again.

'You have to look the person in the eye.' His head extends away from his shoulders like a periscope, eating up my personal space.

Glue my eye to his. 'Cheers.' Slam the shot glass down. Its rim is smiling.

Lukas winces after his shot and gulps some beer.

My stomach gives a small symphony.

'Are you sure you're not hungry?'

'I'm sure. Where does that way of toasting come from?'

'Germany. My grandfather's from there.'

'Is he still alive?'

'Yes, he's in Chicago where I grew up. That wasn't a shady flirtation before.'

'My bad.'

'I want to help you.'

'Why?'

'Because I can.'

'Bullshit.' Smart people are not always decent.

'Why is that so hard to believe?'

'Because most people help only when it helps them.'

'I don't believe that.'

Lukas must have been a Boy Scout. 'Anyway, I don't need help.'

'My turn to call bullshit.'

'How will writing an article about me help me?'

'It creates opportunity.'

'For you.'

'For you. Your story could be a triumph. That depends on you.'

His burger arrives. 'Can I get you anything else?' The waitress has reapplied her lipstick—an insincere fuchsia.

'Jax?' Lukas volleys the question over to me.

With her back to me, she picks up our empty shot glasses. I'm tempted to grab her ass. 'I'm fine.'

'We're fine at the moment. Thanks.' He smiles—his teeth are as white as geese.

He probably has spare toothbrushes in his bathroom.

'He's from Berlin, my grandfather.' Lukas contemplates his burger. 'My great-grandmother had a friend who emigrated from Berlin to Chicago before World War II, and that friend's employer used to send my grandfather and his mother care packages during the war. The employer didn't know them. My grandfather said those care packages helped keep them alive.' He removes the top bun and cuts into his burger with a knife and fork. Offers me the first bite. 'Maybe that's why I keep trying to feed you.' This time his smile is floppy.

'I'll take a French fry.'

Lukas pushes his plate into the space between us.

'The care packages came later. Before, my grandfather remembers being about four or five. At that time, Berliners boarded their kids outside the city on farms because of the Allied bombings. On the farm, he remembers running across a field as a plane strafed it.'

In Lukas's pause, I see a fair-haired boy in short pants, his salt-streaked face willing his big baby body forward.

'My grandfather loves America, is so proud to be an American because America afforded him opportunities.'

My eyes flicker to the photograph above us. The nursing mother's arm is thrown over her forehead, shielding most of her face from view. Her suckling toddler has teaspoons of dark shadows under her eyes. 'I don't think your grandfather's America exists today.'

'I hope at least in some places it does. That's one reason I want to help you.'

It's a perfect fit story. Am I supposed to think he's not so hard to figure out?

'Have you had a chance to look at the rest of them?'

We stand and, side by side, circle the room. I like the photographs for what they leave out. A portrait of a skeletal boy with jack-o'-lantern eyes roped to the top of a train car roots me. Did he make it?

'This one got to me too. It's his stare. It makes me want to know what happened.' There is the friction of space between Lukas's shoulder and mine. 'It's the same with you.'

The doors inside me start closing.

'What do you think?'

'I think I miss my beer.'

Lukas follows me to the table.

'I'm not like that boy in the photograph.'

'Why not?'

'For one, I don't have to wear a Hefty bag as a raincoat.' Drain my Brooklyn Lager.

Lukas pushes his mug of beer toward me. Someone wants a drunk gal pal. 'You don't think people look at you and want to know what's happened?'

Push his beer back at him. 'Only in a circus freak-show way.'

'I mean what's happened in here.' Lukas pats himself where a heart should be.

'Boo fucking hoo.' I am a fractured girl with a bitter mouth.

'You remind me of that kid from Rikers. So fragile.'

'Fuck you Lukas. You don't know me.'

'You have every right to be angry. You lost your livelihood, maybe your sense of self. And now you're scared because you don't know what to do.'

My vision blurs. A snarl of alleys. Then, through a cottony glow, Naji's eyes crank crazy lights as porcupines of fire spread. Beneath the tang of burning fruit is the gravid smell of the souk. Snap. Snap. Snap. Snap. Snap. The sounds of pain drown in the hollow call to prayer. Snap. Snap. Sn— Lukas's hands are on my hands. We're almost the same color. My hand paled against Naji's hazelnut skin when I insisted we go to the souk.

'Jax.' Lukas's voice comes to me as if from a long tunnel.

Naji's flesh quivers.

'Jax.' Lukas holds my wrists to the table.

I come back to myself and smile—a lid on a scream. Outside the window, the sunlight is cheap and bright.

'Here, drink this.' He hands me my water. From the bar area comes a laugh like two dogs barking.

'What's with you and liquids?' Rinse my mouth. Hate the taste of tears.

Lukas catalogues my wrists. 'Now I understand the rubber band.'

'Proud of you're a-ha moment?' I don't want to be puzzled out.

'Have you been treated for PTSD?'

'I'm fine.' Pull his beer to me and drink. 'I miss modeling every day.' Modeling wasn't just a livelihood; it was how I belonged in the world. 'I loved it.' Slide his beer back to him.

'What did you love about it?' He sips.

'The creative play, you're always someone new, and the buffer zone around it. At a certain level, you're cocooned; you know. It's a singular experience. The perks didn't hurt either.'

'Another round?'

'Yeah. What happened to that kid?'

'The one from Rikers? He's trying to put his life back together. He got his GED, he's back in school, working part time.'

'Do you still talk to him?'

'Sometimes. I let him dictate how often.' Lukas catches the waitress's skimming eye and holds up his mug.

Hold up my mug too. At some point, 110% of all servers want their customers to leave. 'You said the care packages came later. After what?'

'After my great-grandmother found out her husband had been killed on the Russian front, she didn't want to orphan her son, so she brought my grandfather back to the city, figuring if she died, he would too. They stayed out the war in Berlin.'

Which species eat their young?

A Mexican busboy drops off our drinks. Wonder what he thinks of the photo exhibit.

Lukas picks up his glass to toast. 'Eyes.'

Jesus fuck, again? 'To great-grandmothers.' Snug into the alchemy of beer and booze.

As Lukas leans in, his breath butterflies my temple. 'Why haven't you tried to fix it?'

His question thrusts me onto a concourse of emotion. Under the table, slip my right hand under the rubber band so that it binds my wrists together. 'Can't be fixed.'

'I don't believe you.'

'I don't care.' Naji's face flickers over Lukas's like momentary static.

'What are you thinking right now?'

'Why?'

'You've got that same look in your eyes as that boy in the train photograph. A haunted fire.'

Raise my glass to Lukas's effort to pin my edges down.

'That fight inside your head? That's the story I want to tell.'

Drown my tongue in beer. He should know better than to ask.

✳

A fat sun bulges on the horizon and shadows spread like water across Manhattan. From atop the High Line, cooler air hints at autumn. Next month is New York Fashion Week. It will be the first time in ten years I haven't walked the shows.

Across the Hudson River, Hoboken clamors with Brooklyn envy. Farther west, in the cookie cutter suburbs of Secaucus, ripe beanstalk girls rush adulthood. They put on too much makeup before heading into summer's last chance to fall in love. Their mothers, with their tugged-on faces, sink into chardonnay and watch *The Real Housewives of New Jersey*.

Farther down the High Line, an old man sits on a bench, his face taking its color from the softening light. His skin is a map crisscrossed with tiny roads that lead nowhere. He smells of damp dust and unwashed hair. What have been the moments of his life? Has it had any abundancy? Alone on a park bench, he's nothing in the hyperkinetic frenzy of the city.

The man's jaw unhinges itself. 'My wife died four years ago today.' His voice is as faint as dried leaves.

Who will notice when he slips away? How long will he lay in crumpled silence on a mottled carpet before some neighbor notices a pileup of mail on the lobby floor or parking tickets wedged beneath a windshield wiper? Will he end up a pile of ashes resting in a shoebox-sized urn, stored in the basement of a crematorium, with his name and dates engraved on a metal dove to mark his spot?

'I'm sorry. You must miss her.'

He keeps his eyes on the horizon. 'Now I do. Now.'

❋

At Frieda's door with my beggar's knock, Don Julio holding my hand.

'I see you took my advice.' Frieda eyeballs the bottle.

'It's for you.' Nothing like tequila to varnish an apology. 'Peace offering.'

Frieda takes the bottle. 'I'm still mad at you.'

'You did slap me.'

'You deserved it, but I regret it.' A single finger smooths her eyebrow. 'Losing my composure.'

'And I'm sorry for what I said. I understand how hard it is for you.'

'Girl, you understand nothing because you're still looking from the outside.'

'Are you going to let me in?'

Frieda's sigh sums our friendship. Somehow, it never gets used up. She opens the door wider and I walk through an aromatic trellis of vinegar, garlic, onions and pepper. New plants hang from antique swings set into the ceiling. 'I'm cooking Creole.' She pads back to the kitchen with me at her heels. The room softens. 'Sit down girl. The least I can do is feed you.' She takes the bottle and puts it on the table.

And so it goes. And so.

Her jambalaya conjures the bayou, and I half expect a man made of darkness to step out from the kitchen wall. We huddle into our bowls and by the time they're scraped clean, we've drowned the scraps of our fight in shots.

'Since you never ask, I've got news.' Frieda smiles with acquisitive teeth. 'Guess who's doing makeup for *Orange is the New Black?*'

I'm jealous and petrified at the same time. I don't want to be left behind.

'Girl, would it break your heart to say something?'

'Congratulations.' Pour another tequila.

'Your narcissism is mesmerizing.' Frieda moves the bottle out of reach. 'I won't be in LA forever. It's just a few episodes.'

'We both know TV is the start of something else.'

Frieda smiles in spite of herself.

'And that sooner or later, your life will be in LA and not here.' I picture her drinking mezcal cocktails at the Chateau Marmont. 'When do you leave?'

'Beginning of the month, after Labor Day.'

'You'll miss Fashion Week.'

'I'll meet Miss Laverne Cox.'

Life imitating art.

I want to be dazzled by her grin. Shoot back my pour. I'm not.

Stillness cocoons us as our shared stories whisper between us. A roulette of the past years—fly-by-the-seat-of-your-pants editorial shoots, exotic locales, the nose candy parties—spin in my mind. I snag on Marrakesh and all that's come since. 'I'm going to be so lost without you.'

'Yes you are.'

Happy people don't tell lies.

'But being lost is a good place to start.'

I look around her kitchen as if expecting a waiter. Start what?

✸

The unlimited blue of morning stretches behind the Brooklyn Public Library. Got a mystery text to meet here about my missing dog. Sit on the concrete steps, watching the parade of new moms jogging behind their Baby Jogger F.I.T. strollers. Such faith. There's no guarantee you grow toward the light.

The sound of galloping ushers me back to the present. The girl with the police-invoking father hops up the library steps and plonks down on the concrete beside me. She shoots off laser beams of vitality. Her Poindexter father must have married someone surprising.

'Hey,' she draws her deeply tanned knees to her chest and picks at a mosquito bite on her shin.

'Hey.'

'You were at my house the other day.'

'I know.'

'My father doesn't like you.'

'Your father doesn't know me.'

'He doesn't like you. I'm *certain*.' In the purse of her lips, the know-it-all woman she's going to be twins in her face.

'I'm Jax.'

'Marlowe.' Her eye roll is impressive. 'Yeah I know. My parents met doing Shakespeare in the Berkshires.' She twists ribbony pieces of hair over one shoulder before setting her chin. 'I took your flyer from under the doormat. My father doesn't know I'm meeting you.'

'I figured. Why are you?'

'You look like one of the Victoria's Secret models. I wanted to see if you were the girl in the butterfly wings.'

'I am. Was.' My modeling career tips its fedora to me and takes a bow.

'Cool.'

'Your parents let you stay up and watch that?'

'Pul-lease. I'm almost thirteen. I can do what I want.'

Thirteen tipping into twenty.

She bumps her knee into mine. 'You're so white.'

'Yeah.'

'Can we take a picture?'

'No.'

Her voice becomes honey. 'Don't you want me to tell you about your dog?'

My turn to eye roll 'Really?'

She bounces up like a lottery ball. 'See ya.'

'Fuck.'

'You're not supposed to swear.' Her hands are on her hips.

'You're not supposed to blackmail.'

'It's not blackmail. My mom calls it creative bargaining.'

'That sounds like a loving marriage. One photo.'

She spins a victory pirouette where she stands. In three years there'll be pom-poms in her hands and a football player up her skirt.

'How do you want me?'

She kneels behind me and whips out an iPhone. 'Turn your head to look up at me. That way your gross side won't show.'

She's a natural spotlight hogger. If she were prettier, she could model.

Hold my hand out. 'Give me the phone. My arms are longer.' We muck it up for the camera. When we're done, I hold fast to her phone. 'Your turn. What about the dog?'

'Give it back.'

'I will. Tell me about the dog.'

'I'll scream.' She takes a mighty inhale.

'Go ahead. I'll erase the photos and then you won't be able to brag to your friends.'

Her ribcage compresses like an accordion as slips down beside me. 'My dad and I were walking near the ravine in Prospect Park. The sun was behind the trees, and there were shadows all around.' Her voice drops to a whisper, drawing me in. 'We hear this whimpering coming from the underbrush. All of the sudden—' She grabs for the phone.

'Seriously? Are you fucking kidding me?'

'I almost had it.'

She did. 'Nu-uh.'

'Yeah-eah.' Her mouth is full of hatred teeth. 'So this stupid dog fell or something and broke her leg and my dad scooped her up and she lapped at his nose and it was love at first lick and she's been with us ever since. The end.' A sudden breeze whips a section of Marlowe's hair into a snake.

'You don't sound that excited.'

'I'm a cat person.'

'When did you find her?'

'About a week ago.'

'Did she have any tags?'

'Nope. Careless owner.'

'So I've been told.' Hand her back her iPhone. 'It sounds like my dog.'

'Yeah, well good luck with that one. Mom says Dad doesn't look at her with half as much affection.'

'Moxie's a great dog.'

'She's not Moxie anymore. She's Desdemona.' Marlowe's eyebrows reach for her hairline. 'I know.' She shakes her head. Another eye roll is coming. 'It's the black and white color combo on her face. And the mortifying fact he's directing some lame Black Lives Matter conceptual *Othello* for Shakespeare in the Parking Lot.' Marlowe thuds her head onto my knees. 'You need to shave.'

'You need to move your head.'

'What happened to your face?' She wraps her arms around my calves and snuggles into my lap.

'Seriously, get off.' Pull at her twig arms, which are freakishly strong.

'What happened to your face?'

'Let go.' Should I kick her?

'Not until you tell me what happened.'

'God, you're annoying.' Start poking her ribs. 'And ticklish.'

'Not fair.' She chortles but holds on. 'Tell me.' She unwraps one arm to get me back. 'Ha! You're ticklish too.'

'I... Quit it...' Fuck, I need to pee.

'Tell me.'

'You little shit.' Try to grab hold of her hand. 'I was on a shoot in—hahahahahaha.' Gulp air. 'Morocco.' We are rolling around on the library steps in a full-blown tickle wrestle. 'A bomb—', snort my words, 'went off near.' Squeal. 'Where I waaaa.' My words morph into a prototype language. Howling, I surrender. A dam's been broken; tears pour down my joker's face, making dark splotches on the concrete. Marlowe nestles her head next to mine to wait it out. Her eyes pour over the bumpy terrain of my burnt skin. I concentrate on the blue above as people step around us to enter the library. From somewhere comes the sound of jack hammers taking apart the city.

'You can totally see up people's skirts from down here.' Marlowe whips out her iPhone. 'That girl in the denim mini isn't wearing underwear.'

The snigger starts deep inside my belly and ripples throughout my body, building in force before burning itself out. Quieted, I sit up, feeling like cotton candy.

'You're a pretty crier.' She aims her camera.

Yet another image locked inside a frame.

'That was fun. What do you want to do next?' She stands.

More like an emotional funny bone. 'Don't you have somewhere to be?'

'I have my riding lesson at twelve.'

Of course she does.

A new idea paints itself across her face. 'You wanna walk with me to the Kensington Stables and get an ice cream on the way?'

Of course I don't.

'We can plot how to get your dog back from my dad.'

'Why do you want to do that?'

Marlowe's face goes through a couple of expressions 'Gotta do something. Plus, that dog gets all his attention.' Her voice is tiny. I see her shy, small self, waiting to be noticed over the roar of the greasepaint. Maybe she isn't a cyclone: all whirling destruction and hollow at center.

Pull myself to standing. 'Which way?'

She knocks her head into my shoulder. 'Follow me.' Her sandals clack down Prospect Avenue past row houses with their swollen bay windows to Kathy's Italian Ice and Ice Cream. The line at the takeout window is five deep.

'Have you had this before?' Marlowe pulls at the hem of her t-shirt to unstick it from her back.

'No.'

'Shut up! You haven't lived. She makes the best birthday cake ice cream like ever. God, I am so hot. Feel my back. I'm all sweaty.' She grabs for my hand.

'I don't want to feel your back.'

'Feel it.'

'No—gross.' Wipe my fingers on her head.

'Whoa. Hair.' She takes a step back. 'Did you get to keep the wings?'

'What?'

'The butterfly wings. From the Victoria's Secret Show.'

'No. You have to give them back.'

'Too bad. They'd make a great Halloween costume.'

We shuffle forward.

'The rainbow cookie ice cream is pretty good too. I might have to get both.'

Bless the ability to eat everything in sight.

'Do you even eat?'

'Most days.'

'But you're not a model anymore.'

'No.'

'How did you start?'

'Aren't we supposed to be plotting how to get my dog back?'

'All in due time, missy.' She whirls her index finger up in my face. 'All in due time.' Stepping in front of me to order, she tosses her hair back before smiling brightly at the freckled cashier. 'Two birthday-cake ice creams please.' What sitcom does she think she's living in?

'That'll be seven dollars, please.' His smile lifts his cheeks before he turns his head to the side.

From over her shoulder, 'Pay him, Jax.'

Thrust some bills forward and we retreat with our ice cream to a nearby bench. 'Who's your friend?'

'I don't know what you're talking about.' Marlowe's face rusts.

'Something tells me that's not the first time you've darkened his ice cream counter.'

She smiles into her cup. 'He's just for practice. I'm starting junior high this year.'

'What do you think you're practicing? Because what you did at the counter is in a class by itself.'

She sings into her plastic spoon. *'I said no one has to know what we do. His hands are in my hair. His clothes are in my room. And his voice is a familiar sound, nothing lasts forever, but this is getting good now.'* She sings like she's in church. 'Taylor Swift? From "Wildest Dreams"? Like how do you not know that?'

'So, you want to know how to flirt with boys?'

'I want to know how to drive boys crazy.'

'Have you ever kissed a boy?'

'A lady doesn't kiss and tell.' She starts belting. *'Just keep it quiet; keep it on the hush. And what we do keep it just between us.'* 'Justin Bieber?' Eye-roll-head-shake-combo. 'Ugh. Grown-ups. How can you not know anything?'

'Taste.'

"Right. Are you going to finish that?"

Hand her my ice cream.

'Anyway, you wouldn't understand. You used to be pretty. And now you're...' She fumbles for a word, comes up empty. 'So it doesn't matter you're not pretty.'

'For some people, it always matters.'

'Does it matter to you?'

'Yes.'

'Then how do you live with yourself? Do you like avoid mirrors and stuff?' Aqua blue cake frosting corners her mouth.

A dot of pain open up when I breathe. 'Something like that.'

'What does it feel like? Can I touch your face?'

Jerk away from her. 'No. It hurts to be touched. Listen, if you want to flirt, flirt with finesse. Don't be so obvious.'

'What do you mean?'

'This is how you greeted the ice cream boy.' Flip my head in a semi-circle before smiling like a jack-o-lantern and thrusting my tits forward.

Marlowe's laugh sounds like a double bass. 'I didn't do that.'

'Yes you did.'

'That's awful.'

'It's even worse because you don't have boobs yet. You ended up thrusting your head and neck forward like a pigeon.'

She throws the empty ice cream cups at me.

'Just because you don't like it doesn't make it untrue.' I sound like Frieda.

'What do I do?'

'Pick those up. And next time don't be so eager.'

Marlowe canters over to the cups and dunks them into the trash. She takes a few giant steps back to me.

'Show me how.'

'It's in the eyes. Look at me.' Make my eyes soft and wistful and bathe her in my gaze. Then I shut it off.

Marlowe takes a breath. 'Wow. How did you do that? For a second I felt like the only person in the world.'

'It comes from inside and it needs control. You want to learn from the masters? Watch French cinema. Jeanne Moreau in *Jules and Jim* or anything Catherine Deneuve.' Should I be telling this to a thirteen-year old? 'And by the way, Jeanne Moreau is not bombshell beautiful. There are all kinds of pretty.'

'Who taught you?'

In my mental scrapbook, Mom and I stand in front of the bathroom mirror. I'm about Marlowe's age whereas time is starting to ripen Mom's face. She's smokying her eyes before going out. A long pendant darts in and out of the crevice between her breasts. I watch her look at herself in the mirror, study how her pupils dilate into sultry only to shrink back into pits. The bathroom light bounces off her cupid's bow as her lips curl into a sneer. 'That's how you keep a man, Jacinda.' Her eyes flicker to my reflection. 'Control.' She blots her forehead with a fluffy brush. 'Control over yourself.' She touches the brush to the bridge of my nose. 'The way you look, you'll need some control.'

Put away the shell game of memory. 'I guess I learned from modelling. You have to connect with the camera.'

'So, were you like discovered in a mall?'

'My mom got me into it.'

'You are so lucky. My dad never casts me. So much for "who you know".'

'You'd make a great Puck.'

'Shakespeare is for suckers.'

'Maybe that's why he doesn't cast you. No respect for the Bard.'

'Do you like Shakespeare?'

'I like his sonnets. So, what about my dog?'

'Shit, look at the time.'

'I thought you're not supposed to swear.'

'You must be rubbing off on me. Look,' she shoves her phone in my face. 'I gotta go. I'm going to be late for my lesson.' She springs from the park bench. 'Aren't you coming?'

'A deal's a deal. You haven't come through.'

Marlowe's face darkens. 'But I really have to go.'

'Bye.'

'You could come watch me.' Marlowe's expression straddles pleading and granting.

'That's okay.'

'You could just walk me.'

'No, thanks.'

Her brain changes channels. 'I'm sorry, but I don't know what to do about your dog.'

Slash her with one of Frieda's death stares.

'I just said that because I didn't want you to leave.'

Are those crocodile tears for real?

Her voice curves into a whimper. 'My parents never have time for me, and you seem so cool.'

She wears a puffier version of her face.

'I'm sorry I lied. Thanks for the ice cream.' She scuffles over to a nearby fountain and rushes handfuls of water onto her face.

From above, birds share the secrets of trees. I follow her to the fountain where frustration tugs at her mouth. Put my hand on her shoulder and feel how tightly coiled she is. 'I'll walk you, but then I gotta go.'

'Really?' Her smile is dubious.

'I'll race you back to the library. Last one there is a Justin Bieber turd.' Give her a head start and then chase her into the sun.

PART FOUR

Night washes itself from the sky, giving way to the vague gilt of the sun. Wake up to the rumble of delivery trucks wending up Wyeth on their way to Tops Grocery. In the half-real of dreams, images flit to and fro: there, then gone. The phone rattles on the night stand, chasing my spooks away.

'Miss Jax, did I wake you?' Lukas's voice makes me hungry.

Focus out of sleep. 'No, I'm up. To what do I owe the pleasure?' From outside my window, a flock of birds gossip with the sky.

'I'm fine, thanks for asking. How are you?'

'Forgive me. How are you Lukas? How is your family? How's work? How's life? Are you getting enough rest? You push yourself too hard, such a dear. When are you going to settle down and give your mother some nice grandchildren? She misses you. You should really visit. She's cooking schnitzel as we speak. ... Hello? Are you still there?'

'I've never heard you speak so many words at once. It's nice. Perhaps you'd provide me with the pleasure of your company today. I'm meeting Kalief, the kid from Rikers. I thought you might like to join us.'

'Did you ask him if he wants the pleasure of my company?'

'When I told him you were an ex-*Sports Illustrated Swimsuit* cover model, he said yes.'

Is in the eye of the beholder! Is only skin deep! And the beast! 'He's going to be disappointed when he sees me.'

'Let him be the judge of that.'

'What time?'

'We're meeting at The Trading Post on John Street at two. Do you know it?'

'I'll find it.'

'See you then.'

'Thanks. Bye.' Before the line disconnects, there is a brief but charming burp in the background. He probably has a whispering girlfriend.

My phone pings, this time with a message from Marlowe.

> Just finished *Belle de Jour*. Wanna get ice cream? ☺

Jesus Fuck. Mothers lock up your sons. And husbands.

> Can't today. Sorry. Maybe 2morrow.

Click over to Gmail to find a message from Aamina.

Dear Miss Jax,

I hope you is well and your family. I write for to say it thanks the money that you send it other time. Me heart hurt for to Naji. People they saying it Naji was take second wife. I ashamed and don't can't nothing.

As-salaam 'alaykum,

Aamina El-Khoury

I feel like mud.

The heat of the shower intensifies my body's palette of smells. Suds away the wake of Walker and step into the hug of a towel. In the steamed medicine cabinet mirror, a face stares back at me through the fog of time. It's the ghost-girl of my first cover—*Elle*—wide-eyed yet precocious. Lean forward, my limbs lattice-like against the glass, and wipe away the misty filter. Half a face, ravaged beyond repair. The pain feels like hate. Two old-woman eyes regard me. My breath twists.

✳

Cross the Williamsburg Bridge in the emulsifying sunshine. Samba music stalks out of Miss Favela's and tails me toward the East River. One night, Aaron and I stopped to salsa in the shadow of the bridge. We looked like two people in a song until a faceless blur ripped my handbag from my arm and was swallowed up by the building blocks of the city.

The bridge deposits me on Delancey Street in the heart of the Lower East Side. Cut north on Norfolk Street to The Clemente, a Puerto Rican/Latino cultural center that just so happens to rent its parking lot to a certain Shakespearean theatre company. Hide in a doorway across the street and watch as Marlowe's father explains a fight scene between Roderigo and Cassio, choreographed with both of them hanging from a barbed-wire fence. Father Marlowe's Converse gets stuck in the chain link as he dismounts, sending his butt to the pavement. A Blake Lively type rushes forward, brandishing a white handkerchief. They speak in the glance cryptography of couples. He lets her help him up, taking in the length and gloss of her hair.

'No harm, no foul,' his laugh is a sad sound. 'Let's try that again. Places.'

Roderigo and Cassio mount the fence and fight using a balletic interpretation of break dance. It's as graceful as it is barbarous. I don't hear the tepid "excuse me" of the woman behind me until her belly brushes my elbow as she squeezes past.

'Oh. Sorry.'

'No worries. That fight choreography is good.' When her eyes meet my face, her smile scats.

'Yeah. Forgot where I was for a second.'

'Why don't you move closer for a better view? They don't bite.'

'And it gets me out of your doorway.'

'Look Gene, I found another admirer.' The pregnant woman propels me across the street.

'Cut.' Father Marlowe turns toward us, his face equal parts panic and decorum. 'Actors take five.' His Adam's apple inches up and down before he decides to cross the street. When we meet in the middle of Norfolk, I half expect him to draw.

'For Heaven's sake Gene, she won't bite. She's not a critic.' Behind the pregnant woman, the low-rise buildings are sun stunned.

Gene squints at me like a constipated philosopher.

'Hi. I'm Jax. I'm really enjoying your rehearsal.' Extend my hand and flash him my ten-thousand-dollar-a-day smile.

Gene's is a milquetoast handshake. 'Thank you.'

'Right. I'll leave you to it. This baby waits for no one.' The pregnant woman penguins toward Rivington.

Gene lets her to waddle out of ear shot. A vein in his neck keeps time with his heart. 'What are you doing here?' His face becomes a knife.

'Partaking in the cultural ambiance of the city. Gene.' The single syllable is a smirk.

'Malarkey.'

Malarkey? Marlowe must be fucking adopted. 'Careful Gene. Your Desdemona was pretty quick with that handkerchief.'

The tops of Gene's ears turn bright red. 'I don't know what you're talking about.'

Truth smuggler. 'Sure you do.' Across the street, the poor man's Blake Lively lifts something from a wicker basket and cradles it in her arms. It barks. 'But that's between you and your wife. I'm more interested in the dog.'

'What about her?'

'You may have found her in the park, but she belongs to me.'

'I rescued her. She was abandoned, injured.'

'She's mine.'

'Says who? She didn't have any tags. Now she does. And they she's mine.' A stamp collector's mentality. He's so proud of obeying the rules. Too bad they don't apply to his marriage.

Stride across the street and enter the parking lot. A few of the actors quickly run lines, pretending they haven't been watching us. 'What an adorable dog.' I make my voice creamy. 'Poor thing. What happened to her leg?'

'She fell and broke it.' BL wannabe keeps her face open, like she's waiting to be solved by another person. No wonder she's attracted to Herr Director.

'Can I pet her?'

'Sure. She loves people.'

Gene pretends to give his actors direction while he tracks every move I make.

Hold my hand out to Moxie's snout, expecting the bark of recognition.

'Oh my god, aren't you the #MyCalvins girl?'

A few more heads whip in my direction.

Shitty fuck. Not the recognition I was hoping for. Has Moxie already forgotten me? I push down the tiny hard thing rising inside me. 'Yeah, a lifetime ago. Now I'm just your average New York theatre lover.' Will myself to blush as I scratch Moxie behind her ears. From her, nothing but a few sandpaper licks.

'You should come to our opening night party. Let me get you an invite.' She puts Moxie in my arms to rummage through a bag.

Inhale Moxie's snow smell as I whisper into her ear. 'It's not over, Toe Licker.' Place her in her basket to accept the invitation. 'Thanks.'

'Actors, places!' Gene's face is a red-hot blur.

Above, leaves scrape against the sky.

✳

Pick my way across the cobblestones past the Schermerhorn Row Block toward South Street. Against a backdrop of renovated sailing ships, the scars of Hurricane Sandy are starting to fade. Round the corner of John Street and see Kalief waiting outside the restaurant. He looks like a puppy that's been kicked too often. I bet he sleeps with his body curled into a fist, back against the wall.

'Hey. I'm Jax. I think we're meeting today.'

'Kalief.' His voice is an oboe. 'Where's Lukas?'

'I'm sure he's on his way.'

'You were a model?' Kalief asks from a place where logic matters.

I make my face blank. 'Can't you tell?' Take a beat and find myself ajar. 'Let's wait inside. I'm sure Lukas will know where to find us.' We both go for the door. 'After you.'

'May I help you? The hostess looks like she sings inside herself continuously.

Kalief looks straight at her but does not smile.

'A table for three please. We're waiting for one more.'

'Sure. Right this way.' She leads us to a wood-paneled alcove away from the bar. The mirror on the wall redoubles us.

'Thanks.'

'Can I get you something to drink while you're waiting?'

Kalief waits for me while I wait for him. 'Kalief?'

'I'll have a Coke.'

'Black Label straight up, water back, and a glass of sauvignon blanc. Thanks.'

As Kalief's eyebrows shoot up, I see his five-year-old self receiving a chocolate surprise in the daisy of his hand.

'What?'

'Nothing.' Kalief hides his thoughts behind a menu.

'I've had a long day.'

'Were you working?'

'No. What about you? Lukas said you're back in school.'

'Bronx Community College.'

'That's great. I didn't even finish high school.'

'You could get your GED if you wanted to.'

I could. 'Maybe that's why Lukas invited me. He thinks you'll be a good influence.'

Kalief looks at me from inside the life he lives. His silence has a texture.

'Here you are. Drinks.' As the hostess sets them on the table, her blouse falls generously open. Kalief's eyes fix onto the wall behind my head. 'Would you like to start with a flatbread pizza while you're waiting?'

'Kalief?'

He clears his throat, 'No.'

'We're fine. Thank you.'

She swishes away.

Do a mental eenie meenie miney moe and land on the white. Raise my wine glass to Kalief. 'Cheers.'

'I hope you two are making eye contact when you do that.' Lukas winks in the doorway, trailing the heat of the day. There are small hamburger sweat stains ringing his armpits.

'Did he do that German toast etiquette with you too?' Kalief snorts with the wisdom of a bill collector. When he stands to greet Lukas, his face loosens.

'Oh yeah.' I get a Lukas handshake too.

'For Germans, toasting is serious business.' Sitting, Lukas directs his spotlight of attention on Kalief. 'Speaking of toasts, I have great news. Mayor de Blasio is pushing prison reform at Rikers, especially banning the use of solitary confinement on teens. This is because of you.' He raises a water glass to Kalief. 'To never backing down.'

The moment is raw. Kalief stares at his hands on the tabletop for a long time. In a culture of silence, you tell the walls. Once the wave washes over him, he wills himself to raise his glass, looking both older and younger at the same time.

It's my turn to look at the table. The quiet is unhelpfully intimate. Raise my head. 'To your courage,' in a husky voice.

'Let's eat. I'm starved.' Lukas and his unflappable good cheer.

Our conversation assumes the rhythm of people who don't really know each other. It hesitates, then rushes at full force only to peter into drips. Lukas scatters words around the table while Kalief sits hunched and tense beneath the praise. In between, the silences are filled by a concert of cutlery. Although Lukas meant well in organizing this celebration, the whole thing is a bit tone deaf. When Kalief declines dessert, you know it's time to go.

Outside, the sky is furred with clouds. 'Thank you for lunch.' Kalief takes in the street, and I remember reading how he was starved at Rikers.

'My pleasure. You know that's the first time I've seen Jax eat.'

'For fuck's sake.' Give Kalief a knowing look. 'Good to meet you.'

Kalief heads toward Wall Street, a shadow pacing beside him. Lukas and I watch him until he becomes a blur in the early rush hour crowd.

'Where's he going?'

'To work. He hands out flyers advertising his lawyer's friend's jewelry business.' Lukas gives a final wave to no one.

'Really?'

'Don't look like that. He likes being down here. He told me when he sees all these Wall Streeters, he sees himself. He wants to be like them, dressed in a suit, carrying a briefcase. And he will.'

Kalief's current uniform is a hoodie and a pair of ear buds. 'You're a blind optimist. That's not always a good thing.'

'What do you mean? Kalief has the determination to become whatever he wants.'

It's time to unstitch Lukas's assumptions. 'I know you really, really believe that, but can't you see what's right in front of you? Kalief may live uptown, but in his head, he's still in Rikers.'

'I didn't say it would be easy. I said he could do it. You know, he was offered a plea deal with time served. He could have walked out of prison a long time ago, but he refused because he knew he was innocent and he wanted his day in court. He spent three years waiting for it because he believed in himself. That's why I believe in him.'

Lukas's words take size from me.

'Do you have some time, or do you have to go?' He cuts me a tricky smile.

'I might have some time. Why?'

'Feel like walking?'

'Sure.'

'Follow me.'

We cut north through the seaport, past Chinatown, and over to the Lower East Side. In the afternoon sunlight, the East River is full of stars.

'My grandfather came through Ellis Island. He shared a two-room apartment with my great-grandmother near the intersection of Hester and Orchard before they moved to Chicago. Even then, the neighborhood was crowded. My grandfather and his mother slept in the same room. When his mother changed her clothes, he would turn his back and see the cockroaches climbing up the walls. Now look at it.'

'I bet some of these apartments still have cockroaches running up the walls.'

'But those roaches dine on Stilton cheese and craft beer. Did you know there used to be a trolley terminal just a few blocks away?'

'Really?'

'Yeah, the size of a football field, with cobble stone streets and crisscrossing railway tracks.' Lukas breathes this information into my ear. 'What would you say if I told you an optimistic social entrepreneur was going to develop it into a green space?'

'A green space underground?'

'The size of a football field.' Lukas is like a young boy with a pin and a balloon. He grabs my arm and leads me toward Essex. 'There's a public lab explaining how sunlight will be harvested and directed below ground to grow trees and grass. The impossible, possible.'

In that moment, I see myself reflected in Lukas's eyes. Turn my gaze to our reflection in a storefront window. We are an old photograph without a frame.

'Come on. The exhibit's this way.'

I am rooted to the ground. 'What exactly do you think will change for me with a bit of harvested light?' My voice takes on a baroque shape. 'Sorry. I gotta go.'

'Jax, wait. I want to show you something.'

'I've seen enough.'

'It's about Kalief.'

'Like you even see him.'

'I know he has scars—we all do. But when you see this, you'll understand why I believe in him. Scout's honor.'

'Aren't most of them pedophiles?'

He holds out his hand to me. 'Friends?'

Lukas is a walking, talking, hand-holding anecdote for everything. I take two fingers, drawing him into the rhythm of my stride.

We head over to a whiskey lounge with a stadium array of bottles. 'I'm warning you,' Lukas busts out his iPad mini. 'These are hard to watch.'

The first video shows a guard getting ready to open Kalief's cell to take him to shower. Outside the opaque metal door, the guard stretches, loosening his neck and shoulders, flexes and bounces up and down. Kalief sticks his wrists through a mailbox type slot to be handcuffed. He exits his cell, hands bound behind his back, carrying some flip flops and a towel. As the guard is leading him, he jerks Kalief off balance and hurls him to the ground. With both hands on Kalief's neck, the guard shoves his face into the floor. He beats him. The video darkens. The second video shows a gang of inmates pummeling and kicking Kalief. It takes two guards to pull them off Kalief and shove him into a separate room. Kalief paces the narrow space as his attackers mill about on the other side of the windowed door. One of them back-kicks it open, and several gang members rush into the tiny space to resume punching him. Eventually, the guards chase them away, leaving Kalief to pace a rectangle smaller than my closet.

Watching those videos takes me to the edge of effort. Realize I've been clutching Lukas's arm and give it back to him. 'Sorry.'

'It's OK.'

We listen to each other's silence.

'How did you get these?'

'I can't say. But Kalief is the one who tipped me off. Right down to the day and time, so I'd know where to look if I could get a hold of surveillance video.' Lukas downs his whiskey and orders two more.

'What are you going to do with them?'

'Kalief wants people to see them so what happened to him doesn't happen to anyone else. He needs someone to bear witness, so we're going to put them on the magazine's website. With his blessing.'

'Wow.'

'I know.'

Fuck.

We drink.

Lukas looks for answers in the bottom of his shot glass. 'Sometimes, there is no justice.'

A small earthquake starts around my mouth.

'Before he agreed to go public, Kalief insisted on finishing his GED. He wanted that accomplishment under his belt before he was thrust into the spotlight. Jax, you and he have lived through extraordinary events. Kalief works really hard so his don't destroy him. That's why I wanted you two to meet.'

'I—' my heart is marching. Snap. Snap. Snap the rubber band against my flesh. From the street, a car horn is Morse coding.

Lukas stops my hand with his hand. The weight of his hand presses me into the past. I land in an archipelago of memories.

'Got someone killed.' Lukas's hand on my hand brings the truth closer and closer. Taste the hard words in my mouth and whiskey doesn't wash them away. 'I wasn't alone at the souk. My handler took me, and he didn't make it back.'

'I'm sorry, Jax. I truly am.'

In my mind's eye, the explosion brings a snowstorm of dead life.

'You know it's not your fault.'

'That's what they say.' Keep the crying out of my voice.

'It's true.'

'Except my handler didn't want to go...said we had to leave for the airport, but...I...'

The hotel hallway is empty when I summon Naji to my room. 'We are going to the souk,' I tell him. He says there isn't time; I remind him who's boss. Order him to pick up my suitcases. He grasps the handles, shirt rising, exposing a terrain of flesh. Our eyes lock. Time stretches. I finger the topography of his stomach. He doesn't pull away. Time ripples. Under the hum of the air conditioner, I unbutton his top button, find the metal head of his fly. His zipper releases the day's heat. I take his cock into my hand. The shaft grows hard and angry inside my grasp. Slide and twist from base to hood. 'See Naji. There's always time.' My voice thrums across his chest while the air conditioner blows cold on my neck. My suitcases thrump to the floor. Watch his cock come, hot and silent and sullen. Wipe my hand on the wall beside me. The room smells of sex and sweat. Re-zip, re-button, re-born. 'Get the bags,' the words fly over my shoulder. Pass a maid on the way out.

'...made him. So...So, I'm not getting on the ontological merry-go-round of whose fucking fault it is.'

'Ok, for the sake of argument—'

'Lukas. Stop. You—just stop.' Talk that leads nowhere. Signal for the check. 'I've got it.' Take out some bills.

'You're not a villain, and your handler isn't a hero.'

Does his ability to recast reality come from being a journalist?

Take a moment and listen to the mumbling TV. 'Come on, Lukas. I'll walk you to your train.' On the street, building silhouettes stretch in the fading light.

✷

The inside of Alat's provides a refuge from the sunburst sky. Perch on a bar stool while outside in the beer garden, gig economy millennials vape over midday sangria, smartphones at hand. In a few hours, they'll return to anything from cat sitting to website design, bartering all their varied skills for the cold hard cash pulsing through the city. Hope none of them are Uber drivers.

'What are you doing today?' Alat sets a rack of highballs on the bar and starts polishing.

'This.' Johnny Walker salutes him from my right hand.

'Then what?' He scratches at me with words.

'That.' Walker salutes him from my left. I drain it. 'Is this how you get people to drink more? Another, please.' Flash him an anemic smile.

'Then what?'

Drink until the sadness is saturated. 'It sounds like a full day to me.'

Alat lines up shot glass after shot glass on the bar in front of me.

My day's going to be busy.

'I pour, you drink. Then what?' He sounds possibly dangerous.

'You pour, I drink. Rinse. Repeat.' Slap down some money.

Alat fills three of the glasses in front of me. 'These are on me.'

Alat, and his unrevealing face.

He nudges a shot forward. The skin around the stump where his fingers are missing crazes. 'You asked for another.'

From outside comes the spiraling scrooge of a siren.

We lock eyes. Will the moment make angels of us? I watch him watch me as I raise a glass. Hold the first whiskey's warmth in my mouth even as I'm eyeing the second. Beside the second sits the third, with the patience of a stone. So what if your best times don't include other people?

When they're empty, Alat clears them away and fills the next three. 'There are all sorts of ways to make life tolerable.'

The shot glasses before me multiply. Grab at one and grasp air.

Alat wraps my fingers around an unwavering glass. 'There are all sorts of self-justification.' Sadness corners his mouth.

The shot goes down like a false promise. Alat sets an empty beer pitcher beside me.

'But they don't work, not in the long run.'

The room become a giant spinning top. An invisible hand pushes me back toward the floor. Grab onto the bar for ballast. Somewhere, a glass shatters.

'They send us to the bottom.' Now Alat is beside me. I want to slide into the inky furrows on either side of his nose. 'Life is long.' He cups my head like a bowling ball. 'Its meaning is in its form,' he holds the beer pitcher beneath my chin. 'No? Not yet? We have time.' He places the pitcher on the bar.

Push the pitcher aside and reach for another shot.

Alat steadies the glass to my mouth. 'We all deserve grace.' Johnnie Walker dribbles down my chin. My cough is rough. 'The thing is,' Alat swipes at my chin with a bar rag. 'You have to believe you deserve it.'

Sitting, I flit into the antechamber of sleep. Alat slaps my left cheek. 'Stay with me.' He levels his chin to mine. 'Do you deserve it?' My eyes can't focus: there are two of him.

'Do you deserve it?' Tears blur my vision. 'Do you? Then drink.' A shot glass knocks at my teeth. 'Come on. This is what you do.' I swat it away. Alat exchanges it for the pitcher. I dry heave and then spew into it.

The bar fills with clouds.

'Give me that.' Alat wrenches the pitcher from my grip. In front of me, a pint glass full of water towers over the last shot standing. 'You have a choice Jax. There is always a choice.'

✳

'Did you know you're silver?' Marlowe's eyebrows caterpillar into a kinky shape. Beyond the street comes the giggling of a fountain.

'Um, no. How so?'

'Your name, it's silver. Mine's sea foam.'

'OK.'

'Don't tell me you don't know that names have colors.' Now her brows arc into How Can Adults Know Nothing.

'What color is Justin Bieber's?'

'Pacific Blue.'

'How can you tell?'

'You just can. I can't explain it to you. You either know or you don't.'

'Taylor Swift's?'

'Guess.'

'Pink?'

'Better. But what kind of pink, Missy? Pray tell what kind of pink?'

'Bubble gum.'

'Orchid.' A symphony of sighs. 'I had such high hopes for you.'

We fall in line at Marlowe's favorite ice cream haunt to test drive the seduction skills of French cinema. The sunlight is a lyrist.

'Christ on a cock wagon! This line is long.'

Choke on my coconut water. 'Yeah, it's a beautiful summer day; people want ice cream. I thought you weren't supposed to swear.'

'You do.'

'My mom never told me not to.'

'Liar. Fuck biscuit.'

'Not liar. Fuck burger.'

'Fuck boy.

'Fuck badger.' The mother in front of us puts her hands over her son's ears.

'Fuck bunny.'

'Do you *mind*?' The mother in front of us shoots us a look. Cocooning her son, she curves around him to speak in his ear, 'Dalton, you know we don't use that kind of language even if we hear others using it.' She speaks in a voice women reserve for pets.

'Sorry.' I apologize to the woman's back.

'You're a bad influence.' Marlowe stands on tippy toes.

'Are you fucking kidding me?'

Mother In Front Of Us coughs.

'Told you so.' She moves her feet into fifth position. 'How do I look?'

Her hair mermaid waves around her face. 'Pretty.' She does. For her. You work with what you've got.

'I feel grugly,' Marlowe pouts.

'What?'

'You're not helping to break the stereotype of models being stupid. Grugly, or gross plus ugly, is the disgusting element of the ugly family and is used to describe appearance, behavior and smells. Am I going too fast for you?' Marlowe overenunciates these last few words.

'No.' From over her shoulder, Mother In Front Of Us clocks my burnt skin and checks for my reaction. 'It's fucking riveting. Please, continue.'

'There's also chugly, cheap and ugly, most applicable but not limited to items found in low-end department or national chain stores. Dugly, or dumb and ugly, is often applied to girl lunchroom behavior, algebra equations and some modern art while fugly, or fucking ugly, has a more general but intense usage.' She finishes her lecture.

'I'm learning so much. Anyway...' lean close and take a huge sniff, 'unless you're planning to do something gross and ugly, you're not even close to grugly.'

'Really?'

In Marlowe's question, there are a thousand wishes upon a star. I see her seven-year-old self waking up and running to the mirror to see if her nose has shrunk during sleep. 'Positive. And I like the Tommy Girl. Good choice.'

Mother In Front Of Us nods her head.

Marlowe stands a bit taller. 'How did you know it's Tommy Girl?'

'I did one of their campaigns when you were still in diapers.'

Mother In Front Of Us checks the length of the line behind her.

'No way!'

'Way.'

'You've done so many cool things. What are you going to do next?'

'Be your wingman.'

'Let me practice the look.' She wets her bottom lip and makes her eyes into saucers.

It's hard not to laugh. 'You're trying too much. Relax your eyes. OK, better. Now look at me and think of a delicious secret.'

Her eyes get doe-like; her lips naturally part.

'That's it. Voila! You're the girl in the room I'll think about long after the party's over.'

'Cool.'

'Now, let it go and trust it will come back when you see him.'

'OK.' Spastic body wriggle. 'Are you getting birthday cake again?'

'You pick for me in case I don't finish it.'

Marlowe re-slicks her gloss and turns toward the flavor board just as Mr. Assignation To Be leans over the takeout counter to kiss an Elle Fanning type on the cheek. He blushes so hard his freckles vanish. They touch foreheads before he hands her a cone.

Marlowe fills with romance and failure. 'Did you see that?' Her eyes ripple. She swallows once, twice, three times for composure. Her mermaid waves fall down like tears.

'Marlowe—'

She slaps back my hand. 'That girl didn't even pay.'

Mother In Front Of Us orders.

'I'm sorry Marlowe.'

Marlowe watches her would-be boy watch his girl. 'Whatever for?' Her voice is a black ice slick.

'For this.' The tickling takes her by surprise. 'Two birthday cake ice creams please.' I order over her shrieks, stopping only to pay.

'Not fair.' She picks our cups. 'Not fair.' She stomps toward a bench, fueled by a disappointment that almost vibrates. 'Not fair.' Tragedy strips her of reason. She hurls the ice cream to the ground.

'Not here Marlowe. He'll see you. Let's walk back to the park. I promise you can rage there.'

'I will never be beautiful.' Her body breaks onto a bench.

'There are all kinds of beauty.'

'Don't.' Her word is a gavel. 'I will never be beautiful.'

'You will never be beautiful. But you are singular, which is so much more interesting.'

Marlowe's eyes remain downcast. 'His penis is probably an innie.' She ping-pongs with puberty. 'Ha! You snorted.'

'Do you even understand what you're saying?'

'Not really.' She tries to knit herself back together.

'Let's say he suffers from deep, unrivaled stupidity.'

'Thanks.' She flicks my coconut water bottle with her forefinger. 'You're singular too.' Marlowe looks at all my face. 'What was it like, being beautiful?'

'Mostly great, sometimes not.'

'And now?'

'Mostly not.' At that moment we share one heart.

'When were you most beautiful?'

Purple weeds grow in the cracks of cement beside our bench. Beneath the lavender flowers lay shards of broken glass colored different hues of thistle by the sun. 'I'm supposed to say some stupid shit like beauty comes from within, and therefore if you're a good person, insert feel-good movie music, you're always beautiful. But that's a fucking lie. Especially for women. Age robs you of whatever beauty you have if life doesn't first. And when it does, you'll become nothing more than a blurred breast at the edge of somebody else's photograph. That's why it's better to be singular. You stay in focus.'

A small smile stretches Marlowe's mouth.

'So obviously some time before the accident. There isn't a specific picture I can point to and say, "There. This is my most beautiful." Also, I needed to learn some things to come into my own.'

'What did you need to learn?'

Images flicker like pieces of glitter. 'There's no cheat sheet for life, Marlowe. What each person needs to learn is different.'

'That's not helpful. Aren't grown-ups supposed to have like all the answers?'

A lot of people do a poor job of living. 'Most of the time adults don't know shit. They're just older versions of who they were in high school.'

'Ugh! I can't imagine my parents in high school. They're such dorks. I wonder if they still do it.'

Your father does. 'Stop. Grugly. I don't want to know. What's your mom like?'

'She hath more hairs than wit, more faults than hairs, and more wealth than faults.' Marlowe's voice bellows. '*Two Gentlemen of Verona*? Shakespeare?' Heroic eye roll. 'Actually the saucy wench is OK.' Marlowe's dangling feet sprint the air. 'Actually, she thinks my dad is having an affair.' Marlowe tries to toss this off but it sticks to her. Her features twitch about her face and resettle into something foreign.

'I'm sorry.' Because there is nothing else to say.

'I hate him.'

Whatever hate is, it is its opposite too. 'You may hate him now, but you won't hate him forever.'

'Why do dads cheat?'

'Boredom, curiosity, insecurity, fear of mortality. Who fucking knows?'

'Aren't you supposed to say he's not cheating?' Marlowe's question is an outstretched hand. 'What about your parents? Are they still together?'

When I try to picture my dad, his face turns to a smear. My mother's used to haunt my reflection. If I saw her now, would she recognize me? 'No. But I'm sure your parents are going to be fine.'

'Are you just saying that?'

Of course I'm just saying that. Most marriages become a domestic swamp. 'Of course not. No one knows what goes on between two people but the two people involved.' Risk putting my arm around her. 'Did your mom tell you about your dad?'

Marlowe clips me with a "Pul-lease" look. 'No I heard her on the phone while I was sneaking her makeup.'

'You shouldn't eavesdrop.'

'Like you've never done it.'

'Like you can't un-hear what you've heard.' I once overheard my mother call me her "money tree" to the landlord. Thank fuck he preferred the convention of bank checks.

'Isn't it better to know?'

'You tell me. Are you happier knowing that your mom suspects your dad of cheating?'

'I knew before I knew. And now I can prepare myself, so yes.'

'But you also violated your mom's trust, so you can't talk to her about how you feel. How would you like it if she read your text messages?'

'Point. So what do I do now?'

'You could come clean with her and risk disappointing her, or you could continue pretending you don't know.'

'Those choices suck.'

'Welcome to the big kids' table.'

✳

The heat sits, waiting for stars. Run in yesterday's socks under a blueberry sherbet sky. Stash them in my sweaty armpits as I Google pictures of my former self, and then Ziploc the socks away.

✳

'Girl, you'd better not have started without me.' Frieda struts up to Teddy's in a pair of denim sailor pants and custom-made turban. The sun burns itself out.

'Lined up and ready to go.' Our outside table is crowded with tequila samples.

She Betty Boops her skinny ass into a chair and bats her false eyelashes. 'Ask me.'

'Are you all packed?'

Frieda's inhale pulses from her shoulders to her toes. 'Concentrate and ask again.'

'Did you decide not to go to California?'

Frieda snarls and fingers her way to my mouth. She circles my lips with an index talon. 'Reply hazy. Try again.'

I'm talking to a vixen Magic 8-Ball. 'Have you met someone?'

'You may rely on it.' Frieda relaxes back and lifts a shot. A grin consumes her face.

Match her shot with mine.

We slam our empty glasses onto the table. The tequila tastes of early desert mornings.

'Miss Jax? Small world.' Lukas crosses Berry Street holding hands with a girl who is markedly but not offensively younger. She moves like a master of sexual yoga. 'Amber, this is Jax. Jax, Amber.'

Amber looks somewhere above my hair. 'Nice to meet you, Jax.' She sounds like she grew up with a British parent.

'Nice to meet you too, Amber. This is my friend Frieda. Frieda, this is Lukas.'

'Hello,' Frieda pulls a spotlight out of thin air. 'Where has Jax been hiding *you*?' She drapes her hand out to Lukas.

He takes it, charmed, no doubt his story wheels turning. 'In the cellar, chained to the radiator.'

'I'm so happy you've escaped.' Frieda uses her middle finger to smooth the arch of her eyebrow. 'Jax can be very difficult.'

Amber and I watch them friend flirt.

'And stubborn. Won't accept help. Almost never eats.' Lukas is enjoying this.

'Why don't you join us for a drink?' Frieda pats the seat beside her. 'If you've tried to help Jax, Lord knows you deserve one.'

'Maybe just a quick one.' Lukas sits down next to Frieda which forces Amber to sit next to me. Behind her head, streetlights shine through the shaggy tree branches, making puddles of light on the pavement.

'Tequila?' Frieda hands Lukas one of her shots. 'I've always found it much more to the point.'

Amber speaks to Lukas in the couple language of looks. Will they have a whisper fight? 'We have tickets for the Music Hall tonight.' She says to everyone.

Hand her one of my shots. 'You have plenty of time. The first band's always shit.'

'The first band's my cousin's.'

Frieda's laughter is impulsive and raunchy and ravenous. 'I hope you have a large extended family.'

Nod to the blunder of the moment. Lift my glass.

'Eyes.' Lukas warns me. To Frieda, 'you have to look the person in the eye when you toast or else.' Frieda's glass and his kiss.

When Frieda and I clink glasses, time unrolls. In its length, there's the echo of a million clinking glasses.

'Or else what?' Frieda's words swim to Lukas's ears.

'Or else it's bad sex for a year.'

'Impossible.' Frieda growls.

Truth be told. Swallow my shot.

'I've never seen Lukas blush so hard.' Amber puts her hand to Lukas's cheek.

There is an opaque thought bubble above Lukas's head.

Where is Frieda's hand?

'Frieda has that effect on people.' Pass out our remaining samples. 'To Frieda.'

'To Frieda!' echoes around the table.

Frieda is the Brooklyn Queen of Sheba.

'Jax, no Black Label?' Lukas signals the perusing waitress for another round.

'Frieda's night; Frieda's choice.'

'Is it your birthday?' Amber checks her watch.

'I'm going to LA for a few weeks.' When Frieda says this, fear whispers in my ear.

'Shit. We crashed your goodbye party.' Amber's tongue licks the length of the rolling paper. It's long and muscular.

'We are just getting started.' But Frieda says this to Lukas.

Amber lights up as the waitress drops our drinks. She points to a "No Smoking" sign beside our table and shakes her head.

'But I'm outside!' For a moment, Amber's accent rivals Amy Winehouse's. She takes two steps across the sidewalk to smoke. 'What'll you be doing in LA?'

'Makeup for television.' Frieda turns to me. 'Miss Cox called me *personally* to discuss her colors. On *FaceTime*.' Pride drips from Frieda's words. 'She has my phone number,' to Amber. To Lukas, 'What do you do?'

'I'm a writer. Didn't Jax tell you? I wanted to do a feature on her but she didn't want to.'

'A girl's gotta have a few secrets.' No one plays the coquette like Frieda.

'Jax, what do you do?' Amber smokes.

'Nothing.'

She looks to Lukas to see what she's missed. 'Come on. Everyone does something. It's how we define ourselves. People need to work.'

How very Chekhovian of her. 'What do you do?'

'I'm a doula.' Amber rejoins the table, whipping her auburn hair into a sloppy bun.

With a throaty, sex haze voice. Figures. 'Wow. That must be intense.'

'It is. Birth is amazing and joyous and electric.' Amber is lit with her own insight. 'It's love.' Her eyes glide over Lukas. 'And it's one of the few times in the world when everyone in a room wants the same thing.'

'If only we could get all our world leaders to go into labor at the next COP 21.' Stars nick at the sky.

'Were you an environmentalist?'

'Amber, Jax was a model.' Lukas raises his glass. 'To new beginnings.'

Savage idiocy. She'll be attractively worn at thirty.

Frieda zips me a look. 'New beginnings.'

'New beginnings.' Amber's chime is a reverb.

As if the force of repetition will make something come true.

Amber takes in my body, staring a little too long at my tits. 'Sod fucking all. You must think I'm a complete twat. Of course you're a model. *Sport Illustrated Swimsuit Issue.* Sorry.'

'It's all good.' Mentally, I sigh.

Amber takes down her hair and shakes it. 'So what's next for you?'

Alcohol. Drugs. Let's hope sex. 'Not sure.' Wish I had some scissors. 'Should we get the check?' Signal the waitress.

Frieda's errant hand resurfaces. She offers it to Lukas as her face ripples. 'It's been a pleasure.'

'Likewise.' When Lukas reaches for his wallet, Frieda "tsks" him and shakes her head. 'Jax. Always.'

Amber shakes Frieda's waiting hand. 'Thanks for the drinks.' She stands, her dress purring on her rump.

'Good to see you Lukas. Nice to meet you Amber.' Frieda and I watch them leave.

'Girl, he is good enough to eat.'

'He's someone else's dinner.' Offer her a glint extinguishing stare.

'There's enough to go around. You could snack.'

Think about today's email from Aamina. Telling me never to send money again. Telling me I am a bad woman. Telling me what a maid told her 'Your heart is a hotel.' Manage to smirk. 'So, Lorraine Cox. Congratulations.'

'The gods are smiling.'

'What's she like?'

'Brave, dynamic, magnetic I'm sure we'll get along swimmingly.' Frieda tames her excitement. 'And you? What is on your horizon?'

'Better not tell you now.' Jeff had a Magic 8-Ball in his Chelsea place.

The waitress brings our bill.

'Mine.' Pull out my wallet. 'Ready?'

'Born.'

Raise my eyes to a gloss of white breaking the blue midnight. An invisible hand squeezes something inside my chest. There is so much to want in life.

✻

Our taxi pulls up to a converted warehouse loft sandwiched between graffiti-clad storefronts in Bushwick. Live Afro-Cuban jazz rattles the glass panes at street level. Follow Frieda through a haze of hash smoke to twin tequila shots at a makeshift bar. She crushes a moon rock and we let the crystals dissolve on our tongues. A slow glitter fans inside my chest.

Frieda licks her fingers and holds. A blasting trumpet is a warrior call to fuck. 'Let's dance.' Sound surrounds us.

We ride the wave of writhing bodies into the heart of the dance floor. On the underside of my eyelids, the music swirls into colors. Let my body follow until I'm my own private dancer. My hips gyrate in magenta, my torso undulates in red and orange flames, my arms float up in a peach-pink cloud of a piano interlude. The trumpet beseeches in indigo before the drums quicken like a pulse before you come. The music slows to silver before the bongos kick in a stealthy under beat. Everybody breathes, clapping. Open my eyes to spy Frieda dancing with the actress Jemima Kirke, who swings her hair in figure eights. As the conga player riffs with the timbale drummer in an improvised mating call, I step into the telltale heat of a body behind me. My ass flirts with it. Smallish hands tulip onto my hips. Move a bit closer to let the rest of our bodies talk to each other. As the rhythm quickens, his fingers step along my ribcage teasing me into a salsa. His breath tickles the hair on the back of my neck. Turn toward my partner, a smooth-skin Latino with a Jesus mane, and we step into each other. Keep him on the left side of my face.

'You're a good dancer.' His voice is a classical guitar.

'You too.' Fight the temptation to lick his ear.

'I'm Pablo.' He spins me.

'Jax.' The band breaks. Stand and stare at the top of his hipbone winking from beneath his shrunken tee. A bead of sweat taunts his belly button rim. I want to rescue it with my tongue, like licking salt from the edge of a tequila glass.

'Whoa. Where are you?'

'Here.' My fingers trace the hem of skin above the waistband of his jeans. Lift my face to his.

His head rebounds from an invisible slap.

My head lolls to my chest so that I'm looking down my own shirt.

'Sorry.' Apology and accusation roll into one. 'What happened?' With a finger under my chin, he lifts my face to his.

Jerk my chin free. 'I don't like people touching my face.'

'You touched my stomach.'

'It begged me to. You couldn't hear it above the music.'

'Come on. Indulge me.'

Thought you'd never ask. Lose his words in a kiss. He tastes of better times.

'That's not what I meant.' His teeth are small like his hands.

'Indulge me.' Move in to kiss him again.

His hand on my chest is a full stop. 'Thank you for the dance.'

Step out from under his touch. 'Anytime.'

Back to the bar to drown in the depths of tequila. Swallow and fill with the heat of the sun. My arms and legs come loose and drift on a lullaby of waves. Sound goes sideways, a rippling fabric of space and time. The lament of an acoustic guitar stretches, shrinks and quivers until the waves fade to whispers. A conga drums inside my head, putting all my pieces back together again. Buoyed by sex and pride, I stroke back to Pablo.

'Hey. Before. What the fuck?' Because why not?

'I don't like aggressive women.'

I am Pygmalion's Bride.

'Girl, be a lover, not a fighter.' Frieda sashays between us. It's the first time I've seen her look old. Her big, taloned hands take a hold of mine. Big fish, little fish swirling in the water. My thoughts twist. The room smells of a hunt.

Time suspends. A man with a gourmand's belly dances like a drunk two-year-old in a corner of the loft. His partner waves her hands as if to keep the music off her face. At the bar, Frieda knocks shot glasses with a man old enough to be her father, but money shaves off a good ten years. All around me, people couple or triple before disappearing into the recesses of the night. Hook Frieda's eyes and touch my heart before wading my way out.

PART FIVE

Back on the street, the moonlight has turned stingy. Walk along the muscular architecture of integrated brownstones in search of a taxi. On Bushwick Avenue, scaffolding veils a church slated for housing conversion. There's a collar of dirt around the church. Its stained-glass windows have been removed already, leaving empty eye sockets in the face of the building. From inside, a flicker of light. Creep along the perimeter of the building until a break in the scaffolding reveals itself. Slip through the slit under the cloak of night. Another slash of light draws me toward an open rear window. Boost myself through and land with a thud near a derelict stand of votive candles. There are quick footsteps and then an ocean's rush of silence. Close my eyes to make myself invisible, but my face is a bull's eye for the beam from a flashlight. Turn my right cheek to the wall. I feel like a guest star on a cop drama. Do I hold up my hands?

'Hey,' I whisper to the glare.

'What are you doing?' The voice is pure Brooklynese. The light sweeps over my body, judging its threat level.

I have no idea. 'I saw your light.'

The light snaps off. 'Wanna see something?'

'Sure.'

'Come to the sanctuary.'

I stay stock still.

'It's the area behind where the altar used to be.'

Duh.

Using the light on my phone, I pick my way across broken pieces of marble toward a skinny black dude wearing a backpack. From behind, his ponytailed dreadlocks look like a sunflower. 'Found you.'

'Hi.' His dimples form a parenthesis around his smile. 'Look.' He shines his flashlight on a mural painted onto the back wall. 'This one is John the Baptist.' In the painting John baptizes a man in a river. Around his head sit winged angels on clouds.

The kid shifts the focus of his torch. 'This one is Moses.' In the picture, a man leads a sea of people across a desert toward an outpost of time. In the distance, sand dunes curve like a woman's back.

The kid takes a camera from his backpack.

'Why don't you give me the flashlight? If I hold it here and you stand there, you'll get a better picture.' The metal cools the palm of my hand.

'You're right. Thanks.'

'I'm Jax.'

'James.'

James snaps a few photos before moving back to John. 'Soon, all this will be gone.' He kicks a shard of marble.

'Look what happened to the altar. The pews are next.' He refocuses his camera.

'What'll happen to them?'

'Probably sold. Maybe scrapped.' He goes to a pew and lies down.

Follow him. 'Do you want me to take your picture? It's a good shot.'

He hands me the camera and I come in tight on his face to captures his ten-year-old self waiting to be picked for a gym class basketball team. 'Here.' Give him back his camera.

'That's good. You a photographer?'

'No. You?'

'Sometimes. I'm a moral creatist.' James caresses the back of the pew. 'Like this church tonight. I came to take pictures of the murals before they're sold to the highest bidder. New York's turning into a city you can look at but can't touch.'

'Wow.'

'What?'

Shake my head. When I was his age, I'm pretty sure my head was up my own ass. 'How old are you?'

'Twenty next month. Why?'

'Nothing.'

James rubs the big toe of his right sneaker on the big toe of his left. 'Remember that kid who scaled 432 Park last year? He captured the Manhattan skyline draped in clouds from 1400 feet off the ground. Normally only rich people get that view. Thanks to that kid, everybody can have it. Rooftops, bridges, churches. None of them should be monetized. Sorry. I talk too much. Everyone says so.'

'It's all good. What else have you shot?'

On his camera are pictures of interlacing bridge beams unrolling like spools of filigree from atop the Queensboro Bridge, his sneaker-shod feet dangling over the roofs of Manhattan skyscrapers, the red glow of signal lights in a forsaken subway tunnel.

'That's the Underbelly.' He boasts. He's taken pictures of a street art gallery painted onto the century-old walls of an abandoned subway station sprawled under the city. I don't tell him I've had a candlelit dinner there with one of the artists.

'Since the entrance has been removed, you have to know how to get there.' His wink reminds me he's just a kid.

I scroll through his frames. 'Where was this taken?' It's a full frontal of the Statue of Liberty surrounded by the Hudson River.

'From the roof of the Red Hook Grain Terminal. It's been abandoned since the fifties. It's a perspective and a refuge all in one.'

The perfect place. 'Thanks for showing me these.'

'Do you want to go sometime?'

'Go where?'

'All the places you're not supposed to see.'

Shines his flashlight on the right side of my face. His breath is an exclamation. 'Am I still invited?'

'Yeah, yes.'

'Where?'

'I want to shoot inside the Loew's Canal Theatre. It's been abandoned since the fifties.' He laughs, he sighs. 'Lotta empty spaces for such a crowded city.'

'OK. When?'

'Tomorrow?'

'Sure.' Maybe.

'Let's meet at the corner of Ludlow and Canal at midnight.' James gathers his gear into his backpack.

'Is the opening I came through the only way out?'

'Think so.'

Fucking great. 'So, do you think you could give me a boost?'

We walk to the window.

'Jax, tomorrow wear shoes you can run in.'

✳

Wake to a wet Kleenex-colored sky. My mouth tastes like the inside of a couch. From somewhere comes the rush of church bells to rouse me from my bed. My hair hurts. Flood myself with fluids while standing over the kitchen sink. Outside the window stretches a landscape of rooftops, each one sheltering a story.

Street level, the smell of garbage mingles with the BO of the city, ushering me across Bedford Avenue. Underground, the Lorimer station is a swamp. Thank fuck the G train's air conditioning is working. Sit next to a man with bat caves as ears, doing his taxes on the subway. Close my eyes and let myself be lulled by the inner hum of the train.

Exit at Smith and Ninth streets into an arcade of scaffolding. It's like someone has taken the city apart while we were sleeping and left a run-down, broken toy. Walk through a lonely chaos of timber and brick toward the gentrifying waterfront of Red Hook. Historic warehouses are being converted into high-end loft residences. Here and there, the footprints of Hurricane Sandy pepper the dead-end streets lined with rusted cars. Trash strews the cobblestones. At the mouth of the Gowanus Canal towers the ash-colored Red Hook Grain Terminal in all its fortress glory. A fence of concrete blocks surround the terminal.

The concrete fence is too high to climb.

Fuck me!

Now would be the time to turn around and head to Van Brunt Street to point at the red velvet cupcakes in Baked's window. But now, I'm more angry than careful.

Searching the base of the wall for a breach leads me to the canal side of the building. A few of its collapsed staircases laze in the Henry Street Basin while whole sections of the building threaten to crumble into the Gowanus. Shimmy along a sea wall over the canal and swing myself under a rusted steel grating, which bites my shoulder.

Past the fence, I can't find a way into the terminal. Standing on the ruins of a broken wall opposite a window, I am taunted by the calm, graffitied silence inside the silo. A five-foot gap of Gowanus-polluted water separates me from it.

Holy bat-shit mother fucking cunt bag. Tit. A dragon spits fire inside my head. Where the fuck am I going to get a makeshift bridge? The day's heat presses sweat into the scrape on my shoulder, which cries bloody tears.

'What do we have here?' A voice from nowhere startles me off the wall. Thank fuck it's connected to a quick reflex body which prevents me from tumbling into the water.

'Holy fuck, you scared the shit out of m— officer.'

This day gets better and better.

'That scrape looks nasty,' but he's staring at my face. He looks like a cardboard display of an old-time New York cop.

'Yes.' Near his feet, some dandelions have grown leggy.

He pulls a pad of paper out of his back pocket. 'You know it's dangerous inside. The stairs are rotted and you could fall twelve stories instead of reaching the top.' He takes a long, hard look at me. 'Unless that's the point.'

I stand on the edge of a remark.

He smooths his grizzled beard and begins to write.

'Are you giving me a ticket?'

'Consider yourself lucky. I'm supposed to arrest you. Last guy we caught got ten days in the clink.' He hands me the ticket. 'But the way you look, I figure you've been punished enough.'

*

Reach the corner of Ludlow and Canal shortly after midnight. James greets me with an enthusiasm reserved for puppies. 'Great. Wasn't sure you'd come.' He checks my sneakers. 'OK. This way.' His walk is a bounce.

We stop in front of the abandoned theatre to admire its terra cotta façade. 'This theatre is a designated New York City landmark, yet the city lets it go to ruin.' I see the future politician he could become if his brown-black skin survives young adulthood.

James approaches an apartment building next to the theatre. At the door, he turns to me. 'Quietly. Quietly.'

Are we hunting rabbits?

His knock is answered by a blue eye suspended in a sliver of space in the doorway. James passes a twenty through. The door opens a bit wider to let him in.

As I approach the door, it starts to close. What the fuck?

'The girl too.' From the other side, James's voice is muffled.

'That's another twenty bro.'

Pull a crumpled bill from my pocket and fit it between two outstretched fingers stained by nicotine. Step into the spilt light of the doorway.

'This way.' We follow our host up flight after flight of stairs. The stairwells are painted a stale yellow cream. From inside the apartments come the sounds of living: water running through pipes as a toilet flushes, someone coughing, the telltale tap-tap of a bedframe against a wall. At the top of the stairs, our usher pulls out a set of keys and opens a door. 'Good luck.'

James and I exit onto the roof. The clouds have cleared, leaving the sky frosted with stars. I want to scoop them up with a butterfly net.

We cross the apartment building roof to the roof of the cinema. James finds a metal trapdoor whose lock has been broken. He lifts it, freeing old air.

'Ready?' He hands me a flashlight. 'There should be a metal ladder and then we proceed on all fours.'

Excuse me?

Follow him down the ladder with the flashlight in my mouth. It tastes of salt and lint. Our crawl through an open duct dumps us onto the balcony of the theatre.

Covered in sweat and dirt, I collapse back and look up. 'Holy shit!'

'Right.' James's grin splits his face. 'So worth it.'

Above, an eight-point sun covers the ceiling. Hanging from its mosaic-tiled center is a baroque chandelier. Surrounding the sun are plaster panels fitted with metal gratings decorated with lions. It is beauty ravaged by time.

'The theatre was designed by Thomas Lamb in the Spanish Baroque style. That's why it looks like a palace.' James sets up his lights and starts taking pictures.

James continues talking as I roam through the theatre. His words come to me in wisps, like catching snippets of song lyrics through the open windows of passing cars. Below, the auditorium is a vast cave. Darkened with age, once-white stucco trims the ornate proscenium arch.

'Jerry Stiller...spend Saturdays...a real education.'

Stop to admire a plasterwork water fountain carved into the entrance of the mezzanine balcony. A curly-haired boy and girl play flutes on either side of a leafy tree. Run my fingertips over the girl's dress caught blowing in a breeze. Cigarette butts litter the basin.

'Explosion...injured.'

Wait. 'What?'

'I said there was an explosion here in the thirties. People thought the Motion Picture Operators' Union was responsible because they were on strike at the time. Luckily no one was hurt.' James joins me at the fountain and takes a few photos. 'Ready?'

We head down to the lobby where the green and blue painted terra cotta ornamentation is cracked and faded. Once it had been beautiful. Blue and green glass chandeliers hang from the flower relief ceiling of the vestibule.

'I wish I could have seen it in its heyday.' James runs his hands over the leaf motif in the terra cotta. 'It must have been spectacular then.'

I trace each bumpy scab on my face. 'I know what you mean.'

James refocuses his camera. Doesn't he realize he can't capture it? That beauty is evanescent?

✳

At Fulton Center, cameras insect about as people photograph the glass and steel Sky Reflector-Net and feel connected to the events of 9/11. The air smells of armpit. Closer to the New York Stock Exchange, the cockeyed streets become congested with lives of risk and invention. A woman hurries to the Wall Street 2, 3 station, pink and blue flowers waving from atop a paper bag. Before she descends into the bowels of the subway, an arm thrusts forward, holding a piece of orange paper. The woman bats the paper away, looking at it like it gives off a grievous light. Kalief thrusts his arm into a different direction. His face is worn down by too much patience.

'I'll take one.'

Kalief slants me a look. There's no entry point in his face. He hands me a flyer.

'Thanks.' Take in an eyeful of copy. 'I need to get a ring repaired.' Spend a moment waiting for the next thing to say.

'Could you step back?' Kalief tracks the flow of foot traffic. 'You're blocking me.'

'Sorry.' Move to the side and watch a paper wrapper being worried by the wind. 'Do you get a break? We could get a drink.'

'No breaks.' His voice is locked in a hard-to-reach place.

Jewelry flyers pumpkin the mouth of the subway entrance.

Kalief's eyes narrow into a snake's. 'What are you doing here?'

Conversations clod passed on inexpensive shoes. 'I was in the neighborhood.' Roaming the streets looking for him.

That snort again, this time more bounty hunter than bill collector. 'What do you want?'

'Nothing.' I talk to the side of his head. 'To see how you are.' In the distance, the sun balances itself on the vertex of the Freedom Tower.

The sides of his eyes register one hot emotion at a time. 'Fine.'

'No you're not.'

'Neither are you.'

Deep water and drowning are not the same thing.

✳

At Frieda's door with a tenuous composure.

'I am so sick of this shit.' Frieda's makeup is smeary.

'I'm really sorry.' Hand her a bottle.

'Is this your answer for everything?' She takes it and breaks the seal. Frieda's voice haunts the living room as she heads into the kitchen. 'To come at her like that, so close to McCarren Park.'

'For once I'm glad you're leaving.' Her suitcases huddle in the corner.

'I'm not sure LA will be any better. Did you know that one transgender person is murdered every three days? And most of them are transgender women of color.'

I did not. 'I think I heard that.'

'Girl, you did not.' Frieda returns carrying a tray with shot glasses, lime and a saucer of salt. For her, refinement is a point of view.

'How do you know?' Then, un-lying, 'I don't want you to think I'm insensitive to these things.' Lime and salt the glass rims in prep of generous pours.

'Since when do you care about sensitivity?' She picks up a shot.

Usually I don't, but I care about Frieda's opinion of me. We drink. 'Did you know her well?'

'Some. We met doing advocacy work with the Audre Lorde Project. Some good it did.' Frieda's nostrils flare.

'It did. You do.'

'Girl, you're a terrible cheerleader. Stick to what you know best.' She hands me her empty glass. I fix us another round.

We drink onto an edgy drift of thoughts.

'This is as good a time as any.' Frieda goes into her bedroom and returns with the upcoming issue of French *Elle*. The magazine is still in its plastic. 'Misery loves company.'

The Marrakesh pictures had to come out sometime, and that time is now. You think you'll know when something's for the last time, but you don't. So you don't pay attention, and then it's gone. 'Why haven't you opened it?'

'I was waiting for you.' One of her nails pokes a dainty hole in the plastic and slides along the package seam. 'Girl, those were some dark days. Not knowing if you were going to make it.' She pulls the plastic off in one piece and holds out the magazine.

Take it and rest it on my lap. Alicia Vikander stares up from the cover. 'Maybe another round.' I need some tequila courage.

'After. It'll be your reward.'

Open to the middle and there it is, right after the interview with Alicia. "Road to Marrakesh", photographed by David Bellemere. It's me on the page, but I'm looking at a stranger. To see myself whole. Takes my breath away. Returns it in tears. Grab the tequila bottle and pour straight down my throat.

'Easy, girl.' Frieda wrestles the bottle away from me.

'Don't you always say, "It's more to the point"?'

'A lady does not chug.'

Turn the page. I'm looking over my shoulder at the camera, the sun highlighting an expanse of cheek below my eye. My once-long hair swings out in a hoop. It, too, had burned in the explosion. 'I miss my hair.'

'The short hair suits you.'

'You're just saying that.'

'Really, girl? Is that my style?'

The next page is a close-up. My eyes are lively, impish. That girl doesn't exist anymore. Close the magazine and hand it back to Frieda. 'Here.'

'Are you sure?'

Say no with my whole body. I have no use for paper dolls. Frieda puts the magazine in her carry-on. 'Didn't you promise me a reward?'

Frieda pours two more tequilas at glacial speed. The silence listens to itself. We drink.

Outside there is the impatient beep of a car horn. 'Shit, is that your Uber?'

'Good Lord, my phone is on silent.' Frieda signals from the window as I take our glasses into her kitchen. Wash and dry them, and then take a mighty inhale. Longing scissors through me. Exit to the living room. 'Ready?'

Frieda has both suitcases in hand.

'Give me one of those.' Take it and nearly stagger. 'What the fuck is in here?'

'Careful girl. You know you don't wanna be breaking something I might be bringing for Ms. Cox.'

If the TSA doesn't confiscate it first.

Downstairs, the driver is waiting by the open mouth of his trunk. Frieda and I hug as he loads her suitcases. The air is heavy with unsaid things. My stomach flips, freeing a million ants to crawl on the inside of my skin. It's a feeling more vivid than color. Suddenly, I am seven years old and my mother is telling me my father isn't coming back. This turns true. Break our embrace. Pain is a wall I can lean against.

✳

The ringing phone is a karmic version of slapping.

'Good morning Miss Jax.'

Only Lukas is this fucking cheerful so early in the a.m. 'Lukas. How are you? How is your mother? How was your weekend?' My words are slushy.

'I am fine, we're all fine. Did I wake you?'

The kitchen window frames a portrait of morning clouds, lit pink, curling like angels' wings upon the sky. 'No, I'm up. Enjoying a morning beverage over my *New York Times*.' Top off my Walker and contemplate the sky.

'You sound tired.'

Do I shock him with the news I haven't been to bed yet? 'A little. What can I do for you?'

'Do I only call you when I want something?'

'Aren't most relationships transactional?'

'Do we have a relationship, Jax?'

Fucker. Do we? 'Budding friendship?'

'I'd like to think so. That's why I'm calling. Amber subscribes to French *Elle*.'

Of course she does.

'She showed me the pictures.'

That must have been quite a conversation.

'I'm guessing you've seen them.'

'Or else this is a fucked-up way to find out they're out.'

'Are you okay?'

Get stuck in an echoey range of thoughts. 'Yeah.'

The silence is a hum.

'Are you sure?'

My heart is wet.

'Yes. Thanks Lukas. Bye.' Turn off my phone and listen to the morning sounds of the city: doors slamming, shoes slapping concrete, security grates thundering open. In Marrakesh, there were the high, urgent voices of young boys hawking tea over the slow, groaning creak of wagon wheels carting oranges. On that last day, a man with a forehead coppered by the sun stopped us in front of the souk to give me some oranges from his wagon, his ash-brown fingers caressing my wrist as he handed over the hot fruit. He invited us for tea. If we had stayed...The length and breadth and depth of that moment run in an existential loop inside my head. Snap. Snap. Snap. Snap. Snap. To have that moment again: the impossible do-over. Pick up Johnny Walker and take him to bed.

✳

Nine revolutions of the clock find me cock-eyed and dry-mouthed. The clouds have turned into licks of flames above the sinking sun. An ice-cold shower numbs the dedicated pain clamping my head. Grab the Ziploc of sweaty smelly socks and stuff them into my handbag.

The Williamsburg Bridge is heavy with foot traffic as everyone clutches at the last days of summer. A gender-ambiguous couple with their hands in each other's back pockets pass an Orthodox father and son with matching *payot*. Playing a game of tag, a gaggle of girls scramble like field mice as they cross over the East River. A pack of millennials making the reverse commute home scream at them to get off the bike path. Their curses are swallowed by the oncoming M train crossing the bridge.

At the Clemente, the audience are filling the folding chairs set up in the parking lot. Marlowe is front and center, seated next to a woman with a face full of contradictions. It must be her mother, who has let Marlowe wear makeup. Did they share the bathroom and get ready together? Marlowe kneels backwards on her chair to size up the crowd and see who's looking at her. When I catch her eye, surprise animates her face. She points to the concession stand and holds up two fingers. Making her eyes as big as silver dollars, she turns to her mother, who pulls some bills from her wallet and hands them to Marlowe.

'Omigod. What are you doing here?' Marlowe pulls at her dress to unstick it from her butt.

'I know someone in the cast.' Which is half-true.

'Who's your friend?'

Cock-fuck. 'The one playing Desdemona.'

Marlowe lets the silence hang.

'What's the matter?'

'I can't believe you're friends with her. She's so gruggly.' Marlowe turns to the menu.

'I'm not really friends with her. She invited me to the party.'

Marlowe flick her hair.

'I like your dress.' It's an optimistic color.

'Thanks,' says the back of her head.

'And you're wearing Tommy Girl, which we both know is an excellent choice.'

An actor wannabe with a top-knot tied like a propeller mans the concession stand. Marlowe places some bills on the counter. 'I'll have a water, a Coke, some M&Ms, a Twix and a Reese's.' She rips a corner off the M&Ms bag and pours them into her mouth.

'You're not supposed to eat the green ones. They make you horny.'

'Figures you'd know that if you're friends with Lisa.' The word "Lisa" is a cup Marlowe would like to smash.

'Who?'

'Pul-lease. Lisa? The husband-stealing Desdemona?' Legendary eye roll.

So I was right about rehearsal. 'Oh Marlowe. I'm sorry.'

'Save your fake sympathy.' Her words move her hair. 'I notice you're not surprised.'

Across the street, the sun's red glare transforms windows into a hundred copper fires.

'And you pretended to be my friend. You pretended you didn't know.' She throws the bottle of water at my feet. A few heads turn in our direction.

'I didn't pretend to be your friend. You offered to help me get my dog back. That's how we started.'

A standoff and then a walk-off. Marlowe kicks the bottle of water and returns to her seat.

All first act, I watch Marlowe not watch the show. By the second act, she's eye-haunting me, which I ignore. At intermission, she makes a long arc past where I am sitting to the concession stand. She loiters, looks at me and finally approaches. 'Why are you really here?' With her hands on her hips and chocolate cornering her mouth, Marlowe is a fierce woman-child.

'I want my dog back.'

'It's too late. She's, like, in love with my dad. He's real popular with the ladies.'

'We'll see. Listen, I don't know Lisa. I came to a rehearsal to see Moxie and she was holding her. Then Lisa recognized me from my modeling days and invited me to the party.'

She kisses her teeth. 'Stalker.'

'You should talk. Still haunting ice-cream stands?'

'Shut up. I don't even know why I came over here.'

'Because you don't want to be mad at me anymore.'

'I'm not mad at you. I hate you.'

'So walk away.'

Her face fills half with frustration, half with need, and empties in tears. 'It's not fair.'

'What's not fair?'

Marlowe flings her arms at nothing. 'My dad, my mom.' Her darty eyes land on me. 'You.' Her feet do a demented jig. She can't find the right pose for what's inside her. 'Everything.'

'You're right. It's not fair. How did you find out?'

'How did you find out?'

'When I was watching rehearsal, I noticed something, but I didn't know for sure. That's why I didn't say anything before.'

'I hate everyone and everything. My mom read some text messages, and when she confronted my dad, she wasn't exactly quiet about it.'

'What did he say?'

'He said feelings had developed, but nothing had happened yet. He means sex, right? Like maybe he's touched her boobs, but they haven't, like, done it yet?'

Gene's slack ass pounding away is a visual I could do without. 'Sure.' I thumb back and forth over the word. Sure. Sure. Sure.

'Then he started crying and said me and Mom were the most important things in his life and he couldn't imagine his life without us and he didn't know what he'd been doing but now it was like a fog had cleared and that he loved us.'

'What did your mom say?'

'She was like "How could you?" and started crying. Then I couldn't hear so well and went to the bathroom to listen through the air vent. He was crying too, and their voices got quiet.'

'So it sounds like they made up. That's good.'

'Except I know my mom. She gets angry after. The worst is yet to come.'

We both look at her mother, who is acting like a house plant.

'Good luck with that.' Cast members shine lights on the audience, signaling the end of intermission. 'You'd better get back to your seat. See you at the party.'

The second half creeps by until the Roderigo and Cassio fight scene wakes the audience from its coma. Following the curtain call, those invited to the party shuffle into The Clemente. Rumors that critics from *The Village Voice* and *Time Out* were in the audience keep the actors glued to their smartphones.

With Moxie at his feet, Gene holds court near a DIY bar, flanked by Marlowe and her mother. Marlowe's mother's fishing-line eyes reel Lisa in, letting her dance, letting her dangle. Marlowe is riveted.

Bathe my hands in the plastic bag storing my sweaty running socks and approach the bar. Bend down to adjust my shoe strap and stick my hands out toward Moxie. Nose twitching, she raises her head from Gene's feet. Open the Ziploc bag and waft the smell toward her. Moxie frees a few throaty barks. There is the clip-clip-clip of her nails on linoleum as she investigates. Take a sock from the bag and toss it toward the edge of the bar. Moxie pounces on the sock, burying her nose in it. Having her smell-fill, she limps her crazy dog circles around it, her hind leg still bandaged. Move away from the bar to see if Moxie will follow. She doesn't.

'Hey.' It's Lisa behind a desperate smile. 'I'm glad you made it.' At her feet is Moxie's dog basket.

Fiction blooms inside me. 'You were great.'

'Wish the critics thought so.' She shows me a snarky tweet.

'Don't worry about it.' Step and half turn to angle my body between Lisa and the basket. Drop the second sock in. 'It's their job to be bitchy.' Watch Moxie lie on her belly to chew on the first. 'If you'll excuse me, I need a refill.'

'Could you get me one?'

Is she afraid to go to the bar? Lend her some courage. 'Why don't you come with me? We'll drink to snarky tweets.'

Marlowe and her mother watch us approach. My phone pings with a "WTF?" message. The next one says "Traitor". Marlowe cuts me with a Mean Girl glare.

Lisa and I take two glasses of pre-poured wine. 'To snarky tweets.' The wine tastes like a riverbed.

'Desdemona.' When Gene's voice lopes around the bar, Lisa startles. 'Come here, girl. Come to Papa.'

I choke on my drink. I bet Gene gets hard in a small way.

Lisa hands me a napkin. 'For a moment, I thought he was talking to me. He is so in love with that dog.'

'Do you call him "Papa"?'

'Of course not. You know. The name.'

Moxie lays her snout onto the sock.

Gene approaches. 'What are you doing here? This party is for invited guests only.' His voice is a tambourine. How often was he beaten up in high school?

'I invited Jax.' Lisa turns toward Gene. 'She's a #MyCalvins model. I thought it would be good publicity.' She strings the words like pearls, one by one, out of the side of her mouth. Turning to me. 'Why don't we take a group selfie?'

'Why are you standing so close to my father?' Marlowe inserts herself into the center of attention.

'Marlowe, we don't speak that way to others.' Gene's pushed his voice down an octave. He's probably repeating a self-help mantra inside his head.

'Figures you'd take her side. I thought me and Mom were the most important things to you.'

'Marlowe, that's enough.' This is from her mother, who stands apart, a fragment of a broken picture.

Gene turns to me. 'I'd like you to leave now.'

'Let me get my dog, and I'll be on my way.'

'Desdemona is my dog.' Did Gene just thump his chest?

'Moxie is my dog.'

'I have the license and tag to prove it.'

Tags can be removed.

'There's also a microchip in case the tag,' Gene air quotes, *'falls off.'*

'You know you stole Moxie from me. You found her and didn't want to give her back.'

Moxie amble up to us with my sock in her mouth. She cocks her head and then shakes herself.

'Is this true, Gene?' The look in Marlowe's mom's eyes could break ice.

'What do you have in your mouth, Princess?' Moxie barks as Gene picks her up. My sock falls to the ground. Watching him bend over to fish it up between his thumb and index finger makes me wish I had rubbed it on my twat. Gene waves the rank thing in front of my face. 'Is this yours?' He stuffs it in his pocket. His jeans are pressed.

Turn to his slow-brew wife. 'I came to your house with a missing-dog flier, but Gene threatened me when I tried to show it to him. I left it under your door mat, where Marlowe found it and texted me. You can ask her.'

'I'm not sure I remember.' Marlowe rubs her forehead.

'I'm sure those selfies we took in front of the library would jog your memory. Why doesn't your mother check your phone?'

'It's coming back to me. I did text Jax, and we met up to talk about the dog. Jax lost her in the park.'

'That's not very responsible.' Lisa hiccups.

Neither is fucking the director, but I'm too much of a goddamn lady to say so. 'Why doesn't Gene put Moxie down and let her decide for herself?'

'Gene, look at the poor girl's face. Give her back her dog.' Marlowe's mother slaps her husband's arm. In her eyes, you can see she'd rather slug him.

Gene whispers something in Moxie's ear and kisses her. Moxie licks his nose.

'Cheater!' As Marlowe yells, blood crawls into her mother's teardrop of a face.

I crouch down and hold my hands out toward Moxie.

Gene crouches down and lets Moxie go.

She sniffs a big circle of air and runs to her basket.

'I win.' Gene is a mashed potato boy. 'The basket is mine.'

Moxie picks the other sock out of her dog basket and brings it to my feet, starts licking my shoes. 'Not so fast, Gene.' He reaches for the sock, which I step on.

Moxie stops licking my shoe and turns toward Gene, who has knelt down. Moxie buries her nose in Gene's pocket.

'You were saying?' Gene watches Moxie paw at his thigh.

Wave my sock at Moxie, whose nose is a radar. She wags her tail back to me.

'She doesn't care about you guys. It's the socks.' Marlowe bounces up and down.

What the fuck am I doing? Am overcome by punishable giggles. Time gets slow and soft—whispers, sips of wine, the furtive inhale on a cigarette. Bring my sock to the garbage can and dump it onto a mosaic of wine-covered trash. 'Your turn.'

Gene dumps his sock too.

Moxie dodders about the space with her bad leg, oddly graceful. She stops at Gene's feet, nestles.

Moxie has chosen.

Losing is a Novocain shot in the upper gums. I straighten my back and shoulders to full model height. The air thins.

'Gene, hasn't that girl suffered enough?' Marlowe's Mom has fire for eyes. 'Do the right thing.'

Pierce Marlowe's Mom with a look. 'I want to be chosen. Don't you?'

✱

Outside my fire escape, the sky is covered by a grey blanket. Johnnie Walker and I are sharing the *New York Times* when I see a large picture of Kalief covering the New York Today section. It's like falling on a bicycle bar. Kalief's patina of manhood flashes in the photo. Reach for my phone.

'Miss Jax, good morning.'

'I just saw the Times.' Need an extra breath. 'I'm really sorry.'

'Thanks.' Lukas clears his throat. From the street, a car alarm wails and wails and wails.

'Do you want to talk?'

'Maybe. Later.' A forest of silence. 'His mother found him.'

According to the Times, Kalief hung himself out a second story window using the electrical cord from an air conditioning unit. Broken by the weight of pain.

'I'm going to the Bronx to see her now.' Lukas's voice is full of dangerous swerves. 'He'd been doing so well.'

Kalief was a locked room, and Lukas couldn't hear the screams inside. Catch my reflection in the toaster. My eyes are bloodshot. 'You couldn't have saved him. Can I do anything?'

'No thanks. I'll call you later.'

Life isn't fair.

✳

Afternoon, beer side at the Landmark Tavern waiting for Lukas. Crane my neck to admire the corrugated tin ceilings hanging over the mahogany bar.

'They're something, aren't they?' Lukas looks like a balloon with the air slowly seeping out.

'They are.' We pat each other's shoulders. He smells of sweat and guilt. Slide him a house ale. 'What? Did you think they both were for me?'

'It's not unheard of.' He sits, a doomed shape. 'Thanks.'

Each of us takes a long pull. The air holds something vague and heavy. 'How was it?'

'Hard. Lots of family crammed into the front room with even more unanswered questions.' Lukas stares into the nothingness of his mug. His face is a vacant scrim. 'They found two empty bottles of his antipsychotic drugs and strips of cloth torn from his bed sheets. He must have decided the strips weren't strong enough and gone for the cord on the air conditioner.' Lukas's eyes lacquer.

Put my hand on his forearm. His skin is hot under his dress shirt.

'Excuse me.' Lukas exits toward the bathroom.

Order a round of shots and turn my attention to the afternoon lunchers lazing in their restaurant booths, contemplating that one last round. Rising from her nest under the grey-suited arm of a man, a woman with my nose and a Cupid's bow mouth crosses toward the bathroom. A long pendant darts in and out of the cleft between her breasts, which have seen too much sun. When our eyes hook, she alters her course. Years erase. She veers toward me until I turn my face, exposing the ravaged side. She recoils and says in a voice I remember from fairytale cruelty, 'Excuse me. I thought you were somebody else,' before changing her direction. When Lukas passes her, she turns to check him out.

The way you look.

The room roars over me. I'm stuck in a sense-defying brain fuck. Hug a shot glass between my thumb and forefinger.

'Sorry about that.' Lukas has arranged his face. 'Did you know this mahogany bar is the original bar, and the whole thing, this big mama piece and that baby side bar, was carved from a single tree?'

My eyes flicker to the woman, but my mother has already disappeared.

✳

Fingers of twilight poke between the Venetian blinds, bisecting my naked torso. Beside me, Lukas's snore is a garbage disposal. Resist the urge to grab his face. Fluff my pillow and find a long strand of auburn hair glitzing the underside of the pillow case.

Lukas snorts himself awake. 'Was I snoring?' His face is puffy with the day's intemperance.

'No. Maybe a little.'

His sausage fingers reach for my breast. 'I snore sometimes when I drink.' He rubs my nipple to erection. 'Your breasts are beautiful.'

He takes a mouthful.

The tongue on the nipple goes round and round. Round and round. Round and round.

He kisses down my stomach.

Round and round.

Sympathy sex could be a never-ending cycle if you're always sorry you have it. 'Lukas.'

His tongue laps between my legs and I'm tipsy with feeling. Kibosh my burgeoning orgasm to take control. 'Lukas.' Extricate my pussy from his face.

'It's okay. I like it.'

As if returning oral favors deserves a medal. 'I'm sure your future ex-girlfriend is very happy.'

He hrrumphs back onto his pillow. 'I see what this is about.' The heel of his hand smooths my hipbone. 'Amber and I have an understanding.' His hand parts me. 'You're so wet.'

Swivel his fingers out of me. There is no secret drawer where we can lie like spoons. 'I'm going to go.'

'Are you sure?'

If this were a Bond film, right now my character would try to kill him. 'Yes.' Carry my clothes to the bathroom. The overhead light is true. In the medicine cabinet mirror, I take in the good, the bad and the grugly. I see my twenty-eight-year-old self. This is who I am. This is where I start.

By the time I've dressed, Lukas has sunk into his own private dream. In the building's lobby, I double back to the mailboxes as Amber buzzes the security door again and again. Time moves as slow as dust. Read other people's junk mail until she is swallowed by the elevator. Imagine Lukas brushing his teeth, washing the smell and taste of me from his face, the room sighing of sex and haste.

On the street, dusk unclips from above. A young woman—half busker, half panhandler—screeches some vintage PJ Harvey in front of the fountain at One Worldwide

Plaza. Eroticism and restraint, ethereality and brutality careen from the guitar chords. She wails of sex and death and pain until the weight of the songs threatens to crush her. Grace vibrates between the guitar's furious strings; moxie drives her contralto. I see her child-self, singing, euphoric.

PART SIX

The room hushes with a flick of my face.

'Shiiiiiiiiiiiiiiiiiiiiiiiiiiiiit.' The vowel sound zigzags around the classroom, bouncing off the brain-colored walls. Scan for empty seats. A roly-poly of a woman crosses herself as I pass, her skunk hair fastened by pink plastic combs. Sit toward the back, next to a man pocked with experience and some serious tattoos. This is a room jam-packed with stories. The old black woman in front of me takes raspy breaths.

A man in a tie, half Spanish conquistador, half high-school gymnast, enters carrying a briefcase. He must be the teacher. 'Good morning. I'm Michael Paul and I'll be preparing you for the Test Assessing Secondary Completion. The TASC now replaces the GED in New York. Please sign in every day.' Michael Paul looks around the room with Serious Dad Face. 'If you want to sign in and go the bathroom until tomorrow, that's fine with me.'

Someone rattles off a shopping list of dry farts.

'If you want to pass the TASC, open your readers and let's get started.'

On the other side of the windows, police sirens whine along 125th Street.

We begin with *Sherlock Holmes*. Each minute takes its time. At break time, everyone bolts outside to bottleneck at a bagel and coffee cart.

'Is that you?' A finger points to a bus crawling up Frederick Douglass Boulevard. I am sprawled along its side wearing nothing but a pair of Alexander Wang jeans pushed down around my ankles; "Denim X Alexander Wang" stretches across my breasts.

'Yes.'

Half the class stands like curb furniture to watch the disappearing bus.

'X marks the spot,' says the finger. It's attached to a sixteen-year-old boy with science glasses.

'Do I know you?'

'I've been sitting two seats away from you all morning.' The boy bites into a doughnut. Apple filling squirts onto his fingers which he wipes back onto the doughnut. 'You look different.'

You think?

He stares into traffic. 'It's your hair.' Cinnamon sugar dusts his lips. 'It's better short.'

'Son, with a picture like that, you don't look at the woman's hair.' It's the man with the tattoos. He turns to me. Track marks scar the crook of his arm. 'I'm Anthony.'

'Jax.'

'I'm Josh.' Josh's mouth is full.

'Why are you here?' I send the question to Josh. He looks like the offspring of people who vote.

'I was home-schooled.' Josh wipes his hands on his jeans

Isn't that something the Amish do?

Eye some freeloading apple filling on Josh's jeans. My eye drags Josh's and he flicks apple slobber onto the sidewalk. 'What happened to your face?'

The ultimate stereo question. A few more classmates gather round.

'Wrong place, wrong time.'

'A lot of us feel that way.' Anthony finishes his coffee.

There is no link to magic.

'We should get back.' I turn toward the building.

'But Jax,' Josh catches up with me. 'If your picture is on the side of a bus, why are you here?'

Think about Kalief wanting something of his own before he was thrust into the spotlight.

Josh pulls at his hair. 'You must have a million dollars.'

'In New York City, a million's not that much.'

Sometimes a laugh is an unfriendly sound. The back of Anthony's head wags from side to side.

'What? It's not like I'll ever model again.'

Anthony's stride is long and fast.

'You sound like an asshole.' Josh middle-fingers his glasses up the bridge of his nose.

We return to the classroom in our own pockets of silence.

✳

Wanna go fall trend shopping?

Thought I was a traitor.

U R, but my mom wants to C U. New Chucks hang in the balance.

I'm being pimped for sneakers.

What's in it for me?

Information. Gene moved out.

He probably took Moxie with him.

So?

Don't u wanna know?

Not really.

U should. Ur name came up a lot.

Can't imagine why.

U put the idea in Mom's head.

No I didn't.

Yeah U did. U told her 2 B chosen or whatever.

??????????

At the party. She listened 2 U so now U owe her. And me too. U broke my home ☹

No I didn't. Your dad did. Plus, you love drama. And you'll get double everything.

I know. Gene already bought me some Chucks ☺

Does Gene know you call him Gene?

What do U think? So are U coming? I think my mom's losing it. She keeps re-watching Gone, Girl.

Jax?

R U there?

I will regret this. Not like you regret herpes, but still.

When

Bloomies, one, Sunday.

Make it two.

C U then.

*

The textbook sticks to the bar top.

'There are places called libraries.' Alat picks up *Fundamentals of Algebra* and wipes under it.

'They're too quiet. Plus no refreshments.' My text book pages are crinkled with coffee drips. Hold up my rocks glass. 'When you have a chance.' Right now, Johnny Walker and I could give a fuck what x equals.

Alat replaces the Walker with a San Pellegrino.

'I've never had much use for the Italians.'

Alat taps the blank page of my notebook before disappearing inside the walk-in to pull his happy-hour restock.

'I could go drink somewhere else.' My words traipse after Alat like a pesky younger brother.

'But then who would I talk to?' A voice ribbons from the doorway.

Shitty fuck.

Brian advances, in all his lifestyle glory: Theory + Cole Haan + TAG Heuer + Thomas Pink + Creed.

'Hey.' Because what else can you say after a burrito ice breaker and a fuck and run?

'What are you drinking, woman?' He strips his tie from his neck in a single flourish. An image of wrists tied to a headboard dances in my head.

Alat reappears, his arms loaded with six packs.

'I'm good.'

'A Black Label, and a Brooklyn please.' Brian hand shafts my Pellegrino. 'You sure?'

Alat fishhooks my eye.

'I'm sure.'

Brian's foot on the bar rail saddles a bit closer.

'What are you doing?'

'Getting a better view.' Brian turns my textbook toward him. 'What's this?'

'I'm taking the TASC. It's the GED in New York.'

Brian shoots back his pour and signals for another. He stares deep into the forward.

'Are you okay?'

'Drink with me.'

'I can't.'

'Why not?'

'X beckons.'

He taps the empty page of my notebook. 'And if I help you?'

'I will be very grateful.'

He looks at me like a cat looks at a mouse. 'See this 4 below the fraction and this 3? They're denominators. Multiply each side by the other denominator to cancel it out.' He curls my fingers around an errant pencil.

'Like this?'

'Yeah. Good. Then simplify.'

We each wait for the other to do something.

'Simplifying is cleaning up the numbers so you can solve for x. So multiply the 4 through on this side and the 3 on the other.'

Brian's father-self flashes from beneath his lifestyle forgery. In a few years, he'll be curling dimpled fingers around a baseball.

'Now, get all the xs on the left side of the equation and all the numbers on the other side. Wait. You can't just move them.' He grabs the pencil and erases my work. 'You have to either add or subtract them when you move them from one side to the other. Start again.' Brian finishes his beer. 'Ok. Let me see. Now you're ready to solve for x.'

X equals 9.5. I did it. Share a private smile with my notebook before turning to Brian. 'Thanks.'

'Do the next one. Start by clearing the fractions.'

I work my way through the problem set as Brian works his way through the better part of a fifth. His hand finds a resting place on my thigh, which I pick up and move to his own. He holds my palm against his taut, hard quad. 'Brian.'

'I thought you were going to be grateful.'

'Not that grateful.' He fucks like a rich kid.

'Is a blow job out of the question?' Brian releases my hand. 'Kidding.' He moves back inside himself.

'What's wrong?'

'Nothing.' He signals for two more.

'Liar.' Brian is a slow dance with painful eyes. 'Can't be worse than this.' Point to the right side of my face.

Brian takes a long hard look at me. 'I lost a shit ton of money today.'

'I guess drinks are on me. How bad?'

'Bad.' He clinks my glass and shoots his back. 'Excuse me.' As Brian stands, he knocks over his bar stool.

'Easy there, tiger.' Catch Alat's eye with an "I've got this" look. 'Going somewhere?' Stand and right the bar stool.

'The head.' Brian weebles like a wobble.

'Maybe it's time you go home.'

'Maybe you're right.' His first step forward is shaky; the second spills Walker all over my notebook.

'Come on. I'll take you.'

Brian smiles like a chick with new, huge tits. 'You are grateful.'

Jesus fuck. 'No, I'm not.' Get my shoulder up under his armpit as our bodies lock into familiarity. 'If you piss yourself on the way, I'm dumping you in your own mess.'

We exit into the tumult of the street.

At his building, the doorman's face is a hatchet. Brian walks wavy to the elevator, grabbing my right breast for support.

Fuck of shit, please don't throw up. 'Do you have your key?'

'Fron pket.'

Slip my hand into Brian's pocket and a smile splays across his lips. Fish out his keys as he plays with my nipple. At this moment, I am just legs and tits and ass. Push him out of the elevator and propel him toward his apartment. Manage to steady him as I unlock the door. Once inside, he flat fuck falls to the floor. Corners slide into shadows as the room drapes itself in silence.

*

Daylight comes in on tip toes. A groan emanates from the carpet. Brian is a waking animal experiencing the world beyond language. Leave him to it while I go into the kitchen to make some coffee. There is a filled fruit bowl on his kitchen table and a potted basil sunning itself on his window sill.

Walk back into the living room and hand him a mug. 'Here.'

'Thanks. What?'

'There's a huge carpet burn along the side of your face.'

'We're twins.' Brian's effort to sit up is valiant. 'Thanks for the pillow and blanket.'

Nod my head. His vulnerability is a comfort.

He eye-thumbs the accordion of clothes beside him. 'Did we...?'

'You're funny.' Drain my coffee, 'Gotta run.' My shoulders give an apology.

Outside, I get studded by raindrops. Head south along Kent to where an organic farm blossoms on a former industrial site, ready to offer Sunday supper for seventy-five bucks a pop. Farther west, high end boutiques and locally sourced cafes selling fatal organic food choke Puerto Rican bodegas and public housing. The muffled sound of quacking breaks the morning silence. Across the street, a jogger picks a wedgie out of his ass with his PlayStation-soft hand.

This neighborhood is losing its poetry.

Back home, open my windows and welcome the smell of rain. Grab my iPhone and let FaceTime carry my melancholy away.

'Girl, you're up early.' Frieda must have just come in from clubbing. Her makeup is streaky. 'Hold on a second,' she wriggles herself into a wrapper. There are feathered mules on her feet.

'You are so Hollywood.' Wonder which set she liberated those shoes from.

'Circa the 1940s,' Frieda smolders into the camera.

'How's it going?' Translation: When are you coming home?

'Fab-u-lous. I may be staying a bit longer.'

Which means: Not any time soon.

'How's Lorraine?'

'That's Miss Cox to you.'

Decoded: Don't give me shit for extending.

'She's recommended I do makeup for the new *Rocky Horror Picture Show* TV movie.'

I stifle a yawn. 'That'll be perfect for you. When do you find out?'

'Don't be yawning at my big news.' She demands her moment of basking. 'By the end of the month. Now do tell.' Frieda purrs. 'How is our sumptuous journalist? Have you been snacking?'

My throat gets stubbly. 'Not as good as you. One of the people he profiled died.'

'I assume not from his writing. Perhaps you could provide him with some much-needed comfort. Think of it as a public service.'

'Lukas has plenty of comfort.'

'No one likes eating the same thing every day.'

And not everyone likes leftovers. 'I can't; I'm busy.'

'With what?'

'I'm taking a class to prepare for my high school equivalency exam.'

Frieda opens and closes her mouth like a fish. 'You're serious.'

'Why are you so surprised?'

'Not surprise. Disbelief.'

'Why?'

'You're not known for your truth telling.'

'Says the woman in the hot slippers.'

Frieda curls her legs under herself. 'They were going to be thrown out.'

Yeah. Someday. Hold up my homework. 'Look. Algebra.'

'Girl, is that a notebook or a paper plate?'

'It's just a little coffee.'

'It's a waterfall of stains.'

'It's still algebra.' We listen to each other breathe. 'I should let you sleep.'

'Yes girl, you should. Calling at such an ungodly hour.' She strokes the area between her eyebrows and disappears.

*

They are waiting in front of the Estée Lauder counter when I arrive. Marlowe's trying on lipstick, pretending not to know her mother, who's dressed like she came of age during grunge. Steel myself and stride forward.

'Jax! What do you think?' Marlowe blows me air kisses from her clown mouth.

'That red has too much orange. Why don't you try a gloss?'

'You know everything.' Marlowe side eyes her mother. 'Ok, Mom. You wanted to actually meet her, so here she is.'

'We've never been properly introduced. I'm Sharon.' Marlowe's mom extends her hand. Her fingers are long, straight and slender—model hands.

'Jax.'

Marlowe plops herself in the makeup artist's chair and instructs her to replicate the look of Kendall Jenner.

As we watch her daughter, Sharon's face becomes a strange mixture of familiarity and fascination. 'I used to have that same self-assurance. I knew exactly what I wanted and didn't see why I couldn't get it.'

'What happened?'

'Life, I guess. Little by little that sense of self got chipped away.' She shakes her head.

'What would you do differently if you could go back?'

'So much.'

I see where Marlowe gets the eye roll.

Sharon watches as Marlowe lifts her face so the makeup artist can mascara her lashes. 'Mothers and their daughters. These days, she never lets me get that close.' Sharon startles when the makeup artist accidentally pokes Marlowe in the eye. 'Are you close to your mother?'

'She's dead.' Sort of.

'I'm so sorry.' Sharon's hand on my back is a cloak of shame.

'Thanks.' Will my eyes to liquefy. 'I don't like to talk about it.'

'I didn't mean to. I'm sorry. Okay, one thing I would do differently. Not have Marlowe when I did. Is that horrible? Don't get me wrong, babies are great.'

Babies always seem a little pissed off.

'But they take everything. I wish I had given myself a little more time.'

Does anyone really know who he is?

'What about you, Jax?'

Besides the obvious? 'I wish I had paid better attention.' To everything.

'Good one. It covers a lot. Where was I when my marriage started falling apart?'

The proverbial cat is out of the bag and gasping for air. 'So, how are you doing? Marlowe mentioned Gene moved out.'

Sharon's face stutters. 'Great. Good.' She ornaments with lies. 'Okay. Some days are better than others.' The smile on Sharon's face screws a little bit tighter. 'It was a long time coming. But you were right. And when he was doing whatever he did with his actress, he didn't choose me. Even if he did come back.'

When someone makes that kind of choice, he's already gone.

Sharon reaches inside her pocketbook for a tissue. 'God, he is such a cliché.' She tilts her head to stop the tears.

All relationships go from the happy start to the sad end.

'There's a moment,' Sharon blots at the mascara under her eyes, 'when you decide. 'There's always that moment.'

Flash to Naji inside the hotel room. Stare at the rubber band on my wrist. Most people do what they want and then find reasons for it after.

'Mom, what do you think?' Marlowe pulls herself away from her reflection. There's enough product on her skin to scrape your initials on her cheek.

'It's a little heavy.'

'Where?'

Sharon gestures all over face.

'No it's not. Jax, what do you think?'

She looks like a badly painted corpse. 'Your mom's right.'

'Well, I have to get something.' Her hands open prayerfully. 'The makeup artist did all this work.' Marlowe looks at us like we should know better.

Sharon hands her daughter a Wet One. 'People don't always get what they deserve.'

✸

Marlowe sulks with her arms folded over her chest, praying to disappear. Sitting on a nearby table, Sharon sings "Come On-A My House" to the wait staff folding napkins before their nightshift. And you thought margaritas would be a bad idea.

'How much longer? I didn't get my Chucks yet.'

'Shh.' Singing Sharon is sexily sublime. I see who she was before she molded herself around someone else. 'Let Sharon have this.'

'Stop calling her that!'

It takes me a moment. 'Marlowe, I know it's hard to realize, but your mom is this entire person separate from being your mom.' Drain the last of my margarita. 'And she is a terrific singer.'

'My mother is an embarrassment.'

'Remember how people have colors? Right now, Sharon is red-hot red.'

'That's their names, not themselves. And anyway, that was so six weeks ago.'

'Maybe you've inherited her talent.'

Marlowe's face fills with awe and heartache.

And maybe not. I signal for another round.

'What are you doing? She's already had one.'

So? 'One for the road.'

'Omigod, I'm living *A Tree Grows in Brooklyn*.'

A smattering of applause saves us from further conversation. Sharon curtsies and rejoins us. 'I can't believe I went to conservatory with that waitress.'

'They're called servers,' Marlowe slurps her Coke.

'That was great, Sharon. You gave me goose bumps.' Show her my arm.

Wine stains spread across her cheeks.

'Mom, can we go now? This is boring.'

'In a minute.' Sharon hunches over the table. 'Imagine waiting tables at her age.'

'Isn't she your age?' Marlowe pretends to count.

'Is she still performing?' Adjust my shoulder to block Marlowe out.

'When she can.'

'Why are you whispering? It's like obvious you're talking about them.' Marlowe's voice is bigger than our table.

Sharon picks up her glass. 'We'll leave right after we finish these.' She watches the servers go from place setting to place setting, straightening silverware and polishing glasses. 'There are so many ways to live.'

*

The craggy cliffs are diaphanous as twilight surrenders. From across a ravine, I watch leopards prowl the escarpment, weaving in and out of the rocky shadows, pacing. They disappear as church bells wash the air. Shadow men come forth, laying down a sheet-wrapped bundle. They beat it; crack it with rocks from the bluff. The wind stirs, pulling the sheet, revealing a body. The shadow men stuff it into the hill's secrets. Only when they've gone do I realize they've just killed my mother.

My alarm breaks through the fiction of dreams. The mountains recede into the city scape as my consciousness refocuses. My cheeks are wet. Twine my legs around my comforter and hump the nightmare dregs away. Picture Oscar Isaac's pillow lips kissing my stomach, which morph into Lukas's with his reheated pillow talk and artless fucking. Flip onto my back and run through my mental Blu-ray. No joy. 'Fuck,' I tell the ceiling as if it could. Beyond my bedroom window, life resumes its predictable rhythm. People go to work, make grocery lists, attend to child care, fuck their husbands or wives or somebody else's husbands or wives until their bodies get stretched and pitted by age.

I want to break something.

Go to the shower where my thoughts are always true. On the Polaroid of my mind, images develop. Pieces of cheap cake on paper plates. Fistfuls of icing. A mother and daughter abandon themselves to frosted faces and sticky hair. Through their translucent torsos like washing machine windows, I see their hearts connected by something as long as string.

✳

The sparse clouds are a flirting sadness. A few hundred people stand on the steps of the Manhattan Detention Center, some holding signs with Kalief's picture on them.

'Thanks for coming.' Of course, Lukas shakes my hand; he's a warm stove of manners. Hard to believe the last time I saw him he was chin deep in my pussy.

'We really appreciate it.' Nothing disturbs the glassy calm of Amber's features.

'This is important.' I wish I were a hologram.

Kalief's mother approaches a temporary stage. She's a tree whose roots have been ripped from the river. At the podium she sways, unbalanced by the contours of life. 'I'm grateful to see my son had so many people who cared about him.' Her words get broken by tears. 'I wish my baby could have seen it.' She pauses, and the symphony of her grief sounds in the silence. 'He used to. Before Rikers and seven hundred and ninety-two days of solitary confinement.' Anger creeps in like an icy wind and revives her. 'His bail was set at three thousand dollars, and because we could not pay it, he was locked up in Rikers, beaten, starved and alone.' Her eyes have the look of thunder. 'Three. Thousand.

Dollars. For being accused of stealing a backpack. What do we want?'

'Bail reform.' The crowd answers.

'When do we want it?'

'Now!' the crowd is hers.

'What do we want?'

'Bail reform.' Amber gives a raised fist salute.

'When do we want it?'

'Now!' Everyone is raising a fist.

I feel like an activist tourist.

More family members of incarcerated youths come forward. Some, like Kalief's mother, have lost their sons and daughters. Others are here to protest the long waits before trial or the lawyer pressure to plea deal. Nobody can afford the overpriced bails. Lukas interviews protestors and takes notes while Amber shows people how to breathe. I let speeches about the new Jim Crow wash over me and sign a few petitions while looking for a discreet moment to slip away. Run into the first bar I see. It's the kind of place where everyone is grateful to be and disappointed to be.

'Black Label, straight up,' and plop down at the bar. 'Please.' Feel like I've mislaid something.

A door behind me opens. Turn to see Anthony emerging from the bathroom in all his tattooed glory. 'Well, if it isn't Miss Million Dollars.'

'Hi Anthony.'

'You're a long way from Park Avenue.'

'I live in Brooklyn.'

'What are you doing here?'

'Enjoying a refreshing beverage. Can I get you a drink?'

'No, thanks.' He eyes my Walker like he's remembering how he used to be. 'Why aren't you in class?'

'Why aren't you in class?' Forgot it was Monday.

'My brother Reggie's at Rikers and he's only seventeen. We couldn't post bail, so he's waiting for his trial.'

Another Kalief in the making. 'I'm sorry.'

'What do you know about it?'

'A little. I knew Kalief.'

'You should come protest, then.'

'I did.'

'Well we're not done. Come on back out.'

Sip from my glass. 'I feel like an imposter out there.'

'Because you're white or because you're rich?'

'Because it's not my fight.'

'You people are hopeless. Two-tier justice is no justice at all.' He leaves.

Shitty fuck. Throw some money on the bar and hurry out the door. Anthony is halfway down the block. 'Anthony. Wait!'

He turns, clothed in sunlight.

'I'm not hopeless.' I'm not.

'Let's go.' He starts walking just before I reach him.

'I have a friend here. Maybe he can help your brother.' Scan the crowd for Lukas. Spot Amber's hair sparking in the sunlight. 'There.' Anthony follows the imaginary line traced by my finger as we make our way through the crowd. 'Lukas!'

'I thought you'd left.'

'Bathroom break. This is my friend Anthony.'

Lukas and Anthony size each other up. I feel like a stick they both want to pee on. 'I thought you might want to speak with each other. His brother's in Rikers, and he's only a kid. Anthony, this is Lukas. He writes for *The New Yorker*. And this is Amber, Lukas's girlfriend.'

'How do you two know each other?' Amber eyes Anthony's track marks.

'We're in class together.' Anthony wears a face somewhere between eat shit and die trying.

'We're preparing for the TASC.' Look at Lukas. 'Kalief was a good influence.'

Lukas's eyes slick. 'That's great. Anthony, why don't we take a walk?'

The guys leave, and Amber and I barricade ourselves in silence. We listen to speakers talk about the loss of voting rights and access to student loans and food stamps for convicted felons.

Reaching for a lifeline of small talk, I grab on to one of the speeches. 'Is that true?'

'What?' Amber applies some balm to her overripe lips.

'That if you're a convicted felon, you can't vote.'

'Depends on the state. In New York, you can't vote if you're on parole. In others, you can't vote if you're on probation. Sometimes, you have to petition the state to have your voting right restored, which a lot of times doesn't happen.'

'How do you know all this?'

Her face scrunches. 'America and its creation myth.' Amber twists her air into a quick knot. 'Voting is fundamental to democracy, and yet you Yanks are so quick to take it away from people.' Her accent Brits it up.

'The people who can't vote shouldn't have to pay taxes. Wasn't that the point of the Boston Tea Party?'

'That's brilliant.' Amber eyes me with new interest. 'The only way to encourage change is to monetize the incentive. What's the TASC?'

'It's like the GED. How's the child birth business?'

'Great. I've decided I want to know more about the other end, so I'm training to become a death doula.'

'A what?'

'You provide emotional support for the dying and their families. It makes sense. I mean, we know what the birthing process looks like, but we don't really know what someone who's actively dying looks like. You should see it...'

Amber's lips are moving, but all I hear is the slow-motion ferocity of the explosion in Marrakesh. Naji's face strobes off and on inside my head. Touch the rubber band around my wrist. I am standing on a Manhattan sidewalk. Focus on the tip of Amber's tongue, which is the color of deli meat.

'...their breathing sounds different. There's a serenity.' She pauses, and we both wait for me to say something.

'Have you been in the room when a person actually dies?'

'Yeah. It was trippy. Voyeuristic and intrusive but also profound. There wasn't this poltergeist of energy, but there was a moment of, well, grace. I haven't completely wrapped my head around it.' Amber fluoresces. 'You know, it's the most worthwhile thing I do. Even if I never talk to the person I'm attending, I know I bring them some comfort.'

I should have slept with Amber instead of Lukas. 'What about you? Doesn't it fuck with your head?'

'That first guy did. But the training and volunteering make me a lot less afraid of dying.'

'I never think about dying.'

Amber's mouth falls open.

It's not the best look for her. 'What?'

'Nothing.' Her body is seized with silence.

'Bullshit. What?'

'Nothing.' She rummages through her messenger bag.

Yank on her purse strap. 'Then take your face out of your bag and look at me.'

'Lukas hinted you might be self-destructive.'

Did he?

'I mean, it's understandable. After the accident, with your career over and your face...But I don't think you'd ever do it. You love yourself too much.'

I am standing at the edge of a humiliating interior quicksand.

'I didn't mean it like, like you're a narcissist. I meant it in a healthy "You respect yourself" kind of frame.'

I step over it into a clearing of rage.

'Oh God, Jax. The expression on your face. Please, say something.'

'Now I am sorry and not sorry I slept with your boyfriend. How self-destructive of me. But you know Lukas.' Look her up and down against some conscious criteria. 'He loves a project.' Even as her face looms red and tear-stained and splotchy, Amber is fading, like a passing car in the rearview mirror: smaller, larger, then gone.

✸

Anthony hands me a coffee under an unrelenting sun. 'What happened to you yesterday? When Lukas and I got back, both you and Amber were gone.'

My thoughts pour from drink to drink, backwards through the evening, to the afternoon and Amber's face. I want another shower. 'Nothing.' An underachieving muffler scrapes its way up the street. 'Got tired and went home.'

'You look like shit.' Anthony refuses my money.

'Then my outside matches my inside.' Watch Josh gulp down some juice, mesmerized by his pistoning Adam's apple. Some malevolent force cinches the metal corset around my head a notch tighter. 'Fuck, this is going to be a long class.'

'Go home. I'll take notes for you.'

'I'm already here.'

'Punishing yourself won't make up for it.'

'The history of Christianity might disagree with you.' Stare as Josh stuffs half a Long John in his mouth.

Anthony pivots, blocking my view of Josh. 'The only thing that will make you feel better is not to do it in the first place. Do you know why you drink?'

Is this a trick question? 'Because I'm fucking thirsty. Do you mind? Personal space.' I want to see what Josh eats next.

Anthony sidesteps without skipping a beat. 'You need to figure out the why before you can conquer your addiction.'

'I'm not an addict.'

'Alcoholic. Same thing.'

'I'm not an alcoholic.'

'How often do you drink?'

Every day. Since the accident. 'It depends. Jesus fuck!' Josh is unwrapping a Snickers. Anthony's glance grazes past Josh before it cuts back into me. His eyes hurt. How did Anthony become?

'How often are you hungover?'

'Maybe once a week.' Give or take.

'Does that seem normal to you?'

'Yes. I'm young and single, and I live in New York City.'

'It's not normal.'

'Neither is a lascivious Cheeto running for president, yet here we are.'

'I dare you not to drink for a week.'

'Why would I do that?'

'To see if you can.'

'Of course, I can. I don't want to. Why would I stop doing something that makes me happy?'

'It doesn't make you happy.'

'I love when people tell me how I feel.' Wash down some Advil with my coffee. 'And not drinking for a week wouldn't prove I'm not an alcoholic. Which I'm not.'

'You might learn something about yourself. You could pay attention to how you feel or what's happening around you when you want to drink. You could write it down.'

That is way too much work.

'So, what do you think?'

'I think dear diary-ing about my non-problematic drinking habits is going to fuck me off worse than yoga does.'

'So, you'll try it.'

'You start a lot of sentences with "so". I said I could. I didn't say I would.'

'You're right. You said you could. So, I'm saying prove it.'

'Why do you care?'

'I've been you.'

There's a stone in my throat. 'How will you know I haven't cheated?'

'I trust you. And I know you want to learn something about yourself.'

'No, I don't.' Peer up at his hard soft mouth. 'Starting from when?'

'Right now. Next Tuesday you can drink again. The loser takes the winner to Sylvia's after class.'

We shake. Does Anthony have witchy powers or what?

✳

Outside the air is like cucumbers. Approach Alat's with its teeming bar. A few holdouts sit in the garden, wrapped in plaid blankets. Packed in among his crew, Brian trades shots with the female waitstaff from Teddy's. My mouth waters. Everyone sits in twos or threes. Stick to the dark until I turn a corner and wander into the anonymity of a forgotten side street. Garbage from a dumpster overflows onto the curb. A steady and then quickened tapping interrupts the loop of Guns 'N Roses' "Patience" playing inside my head. Across the street, a man sits on plastic chair poised over a classical guitar as if it were a lover's body. The tapping stops, abutting a wall of silence. He strums the guitar, notes cascading from the strings as he fingers the in-between. In front of him, a woman, cigarette dangling from her lips, carves the air with her fingertips. Then, her feet beat a relentless staccato into the pavement. She slaps her thighs and her body goes rigid with silence. The cry of the guitar coaxes her heels into stamping, her fingers into snapping, until she is using every part of herself to dance what cannot be said. Sound and silence narrate the story as she dances on language. There is passion and pathos and odyssey in the elongated curve of her spine. As her limbs arabesque, something ineffable radiates from the dancer's breaking points. I am pulled into communion with the anguish of her naked inner being. Released, the dancer lifts her head and struts off into the shadows. All that remains is her life force, vivifying the cityscape with abandon.

✳

Sharon sports a choppy lob. She's also got new highlights and a fresh manicure. Somebody's getting a divorce.

'How long have you been waiting?' She wafts of fresh shampoo.

For about half a jug of sangria. 'Not long. You look great.'

'Thanks.' She smiles the type of smile people have when they are trying something new. As Sharon takes in the small stage a few feet in front of us, another kind of smile pulls her face. It's the kind of smile people have when they realize what they've been missing.

'Sangria?' Pour before she answers.

'Thanks. Great place.'

'Yeah, its namesake is a larger-than-life woman who used to give out dimes and bars of soap to the bums on the Bowery during the Depression.' Raise my glass to the rough angel. 'And it has live flamenco on select evenings.'

'I love that. Speaking of bums, I had my first date since Gene moved out.'

'How'd it go?'

'Disappointingly. That's the last time I go out with someone I've seen only in a suit.'

'What happened?'

'Let's just say that if someone is not invested in a sit-up routine, I'm probably not going to want to have sex with him.'

'With that attitude of female sexual entitlement, you shouldn't whisper "have sex with him." Say "Fuck".' I hit the plosive hard. 'Come on, give me a "fuck". Are you blushing?'

Sharon's face is a comedy/tragedy mask. She carefully tilts back her head. 'I'm okay. Just give me a minute.' She takes a few breaths. 'Sorry. I realized that I'm thirty-six years old, and I've barely had any good sex in my life.'

Strike a concerned look for Sharon's sake.

'And Gene has someone almost half his age on her knees. Part of me needs to get even.'

Nothing good comes from anger fucking.

'He made a fool out of me.'

Love and ego are incompatible.

'I've had four lovers in my whole life.' Sharon refills her glass. 'Pathetic, right?'

Not as bad as being conceived behind a gravitron, but still. 'She only blew him to help her career. You know that. And you will have great sex again.' Sure.

'Yeah,' but Sharon's unconvinced. 'Of course I'm not really this shallow, but I would like to have a strapping man to crawl around on. God, I've got to stop watching *Outlander*.' She looks at her hand where a ring used to be. 'I can't believe I was married for almost fourteen years.'

'Holy shit. You got married young.'

'It was right after 9/11. I needed something steady in all that confusion. Gene was my first love, so I married him.' Sharon contemplates the room. 'Remember being fourteen, and how terrifying and perfect it was to be kissed by an older boy? Marlowe has all that in front of her. Sometimes, all I see in front of me is empty space.'

'Thirty-six is not an unfuckable age.' Flag the flitting waitress. 'Two Black Labels straight up, please.'

'Not for me.'

'I know.' Reassure the waitress. 'Two please.'

'What about you? Your life was so glamorous. You must have had a great love.'

Women are fattened on the promise of love. Do pretty people love more deeply? Maybe themselves. 'One or two. Love changes with context. Most of the time I had sex pretending to be love. You'll see after you've been dating for a while.'

'What's it like for you now?'

Post face. 'Sex isn't the height of intimacy.'

Sharon looks as if she thinks it is. 'What about love?'

Cinderella got a makeover. Sleeping was a beauty. Love isn't possible for people who look like me. 'Love is an emotional ambition.'

'I wonder how many people here are happily married.'

I wonder how many people here are happily married but out on a date with someone else.

'Should I have taken him back?'

'No one can answer that for you, but I would take that energy you're spending on him and put it into getting what you want.'

'You're right.'

'Never take my advice.' Pour out the jug in her glass. 'There are going to be some hard moments.'

'I know.'

'And that is why we have the solace of alcohol.' Shoot back both pours. 'And then those moments go away, and you'll be glad you made the decision you made.'

The shit we say because we need to hear it. Decisions are neither bad nor good. It's the consequences that make them so. Sharon and I take a break from speaking and watch the crowd.

A man and a woman file onto the stage, the man carrying a guitar. They sit on small wooden chairs and the man teases the guitar strings, filling the air with unfinished thoughts. With closed eyes, the woman opens her mouth, her uncaged voice longing for and afraid of form. The sound stills the room. Her mouth shuts and the room crashes on a wave of silence. The man plays again, the notes rollicking beneath his fingertips until the woman is drawn to play. The man's strumming becomes more urgent until the woman rises, singing, her hands begging air out of her chest. Elegance drapes her pain. Sharon is transfixed. Now the woman turns to the salvaged wood walls, beating a rhythm against her heart. The guitar carries her softly until once again she turns toward the audience and sings with the urgency of living. Spent, she sits, clapping.

The clapping conjures a dancer from the shadows. She has the thick, hard fat of an active middle-aged woman. She poises herself center stage before arching her back, her arms suspended, hands like birds, and turns with wild precision, the red ruffled train of her dress creating a whirlpool of rose petals on the floor. One by one, notes are plucked from the guitar; forming a trellis for the dancer's fingers. High above her head, her fingers become the fulcrum of her spinning. Castanets punctuate her twirls as she transforms into a cyclone of sound. There is nothing but hands and feet and primal rhythmic euphoria. Her arms lower, her body moving with force but also with lightness. The center of her being lodges inside her mesmerizing hips, which dip and sway, and stop and turn unpredictably, like life. Dancing releases everything in her that is coarse, transforming her into a furl of beauty.

✳

The classroom smells of damp wool and cigarette smoke. Anthony proofreads his essay at a desk covered in math equations. Move a coffee into his view. 'Here.'

'Thanks.' He barely looks up from his paragraph.

Read over his shoulder. It's an argumentative essay on the problems of using solitary confinement as a rehabilitation method. Anthony never mentions his brother, instead citing a study by University of Toronto professor Brett Story. 'That's really good. Did Lukas think he could help your brother?'

'He was sympathetic but didn't see anything new. Kalief is a story. My brother is a statistic.'

'I'm sorry.'

'What did you write about?'

'Abolishing federal and state income tax for convicted felons that have lost their voting rights.' Give a shit-eating grin. 'It's my activist awakening.' Where's my reform orgasm?

'That's the first time I've seen you smile for real. You look like a little girl.'

My face gets hot. 'Thanks. Now I feel bad for the next thing I'm going to say. Lunch is on me tomorrow.'

'What happened?' Anthony keeps a neutral face.

'Nothing. Went out with a friend and had a few drinks.' And went home by myself and had a few more.

Anthony goes back to his paper. 'I'll make sure I come real hungry.'

Is that it?

He glances up with his see-through eyes. 'I want to finish checking this. Thanks for the coffee.'

My face burns as I walk over to my desk. Josh is sitting next to it watching an ISIS "how to" execution video on his iPhone. 'Nice haircut.' Some cool girl must have taken him under her wing.

'Thanks. Oh man!' Josh looks away from his phone.

'Why do you watch that shit?'

'Because it's there.' His persona of teenage nonchalance hasn't gelled yet.

Michael Paul enters and takes attendance. In the weeks we've been in session, our numbers have halved. 'I'll take your papers.'

About a third of us hand something in. Michael Paul moves on to the Syrian refugee crisis. As he lectures, it's easy to tell which students are undocumented and which are not. Using our notes, we hold a mock debate on whether the US should accept more refugees than it currently does. We wind up drowning one another in language. The class ends on a high, each of us thinking we've solved the world's problems. Decide to wait for Anthony outside.

'Are you mad at me?'

'Why would I be?' He continues past me, headed uptown.

Catch up with him. 'Because I drank. Can you stop moving for a second?'

'Sorry, gotta get to work. Not all of us have a million dollars.'

'I am so sick of hearing that.' Truth is, I have no idea what I'm worth.

'Nice problem to have.'

'Anthony, look at my face. I have problems.'

'Jax, you have no idea what problems are.' There's a cold varnish to his eyes.

'You have no fucking right to say that to me.'

'Besides drinking and hanging out, what do you do?'

I get people killed. Across the street, a shrunken old woman clutching a cane shuffles along the broken sidewalk. Part of me wants to trip her.

'How do you make this world a better place?'

'Fuck you, Anthony. Like you made the world a better place when you were sticking all those needles in your arm.' Start to cross the street to where a bus is lightening its load.

'Don't walk away.' Anthony grabs my arm.

Smack his stubborn fingers. 'Get off me.'

'Jax, stop. Do you even know where that bus is going? Look, you're not the only one wrestling with mistakes, but you need to own them.'

'I fucking own them Anthony, and it doesn't undo them.' My tears come hot and fast. Hide them in my shoulder. Anthony waits them out. 'Sorry for my needle comment.'

'It was true.'

'Not my place to say it. Look, I don't want to make you late for work. Let me give you cab fare.'

'Jax.' He uses the type of voice that makes sure I'm listening. 'You can't buy off guilt, and you can't drink it away.'

'What the fuck do you do with it?'

'Having something to do helps. So does having community. It's okay to need other people.'

I get stuck somewhere between cruelty and tenderness. Speak through a rictus of a smile. 'I should let you go. Don't forget to come hungry tomorrow.' Farther up the block, that old lady with the cane is still standing.

✳

Watery Brooklyn sunlight falls over my bed, accompanying the apocalyptic truck traffic of morning. My future stretches forth like a barren, dusty road. In the kitchen, Johnny Walker wishes me a good morning before I get on Google.

Dress quickly and hurry to the L train with the hope of outrunning the ache inside me. The platform is more crowded than Alat's at happy hour. Three Manhattan-bound trains pass before I'm able to join the sardine of people smashed inside a subway car. A few people crank their necks to stare, becoming a human picture frame that sets off my disfigurement.

The train belches us out at Union Square. Trail an old man with a bitter walk to the down town six train. His meek, thrown back shoulders work hard to upright his chest. Hearing aids protrude from both his ears. For him, is the noise so thick that all he hears is silence?

Back outside into a half-hearted rain. Stop at my bank before making my way through the run-down streets of Chinatown to Center Street and the bail window of the Manhattan Detention Complex through an ashtray of a parking lot. Knock on the window and use my face to get someone's attention. Wait until a woman with geometric eyebrows opens the window. She gives a little yelp. 'Can I help you?' Her breath gums our faces together.

Feel like a cocktail party liberal. 'I'd like to post bail for someone at Rikers.'

She buzzes open the door. Inside smells of the history of man. Two young boys run helter-skelter along the scarred linoleum. The bigger one trips the littler one, just because. The little one goes down in a heap, tears streaming down his confused, orphaned face. His crying grows aggressive until the bigger ones gives a sadistic smile. No one seems in charge. Along the wall opposite a counter, a lonely border of plastic chairs are filled. Near the corner, a girl hidden in a hoodie changes her baby's diaper with twig fingers. The baby swims her legs, taking in the room with low stakes curiosity.

The woman with the eyebrows pulls me back to attention. 'Name?'

The question moves in two directions. 'Mine or the inmate's? Because I'd like to post it anonymously.'

'The inmate's.'

Shit, what is Anthony's last name? In my mind's eye, I read it from the top of his solitary confinement essay. 'Duncan. D-U-N-C-A-N.'

'We got a lot of Duncans. You got a first name?'

'Rrrr,' my lips thin.

'You don't know?'

'He's my friend's brother.'

Her exhale is long and loud.

'Reggie.' The name erupts from my mouth.

Her stiletto acrylics clatter against the computer keys. 'I have a Reggie Duncan, a Ronald Eric Duncan and a Reginald Washington Duncan. Which one?'

'Are family members listed? My friend's name is Anthony.'

'Not on this database.'

'Can you check by year of birth? My Reggie is seventeen.'

'Two were born in 1998; the third in 1990.'

Fuck nuts. 'How much for both of the 1998s?'

'Eleven thousand dollars.'

Jesus fuck. 'Which ones were born in 1998?'

'I can't give out specific, personal information. Why don't you call your friend?'

'I can't.' Literally, because I don't have his phone number.

'I'm sorry.' She isn't. 'But I don't have time for games.'

'I have money.' Scrabble inside my bag and pull out a rubber band of bills. 'I can pay.' I must look like a drug dealer. 'You don't have to give out information. Can you confirm or deny?' Hanging out with Lukas has finally had an advantage. 'Reginald Washington Duncan was born in 1998.' They say hope equals confidence plus desire. 'Please.'

She swallows with deliberation. 'Confirm.'

'Reggie Duncan was born in 1998.'

'Deny.'

'Ok. I will start with Reginald Washington Duncan. How much for him alone?'

'Five thousand five hundred.'

Give myself a small little laugh. It's the kind of laugh people have when they are doing something good. Start to count out bills. 'I used to be a model.'

'Put your money away, Cindy Crawford, and fill out this form.'

The paper has "Surety Information" printed across the top. Take a quick glance at the questions. 'I don't have this information.'

For a moment, she disappears behind a curtain of hands. Did she just mutter "white people"? When she speaks next, her voice has a false bottom. 'Go to the Department of Corrections Lookup and find your friend's profile. Take the information from there. Then bring the form back to me.'

Pull out my phone.

'Not at my counter.'

Find an empty spot along a wall and start writing. A few heads regard me with so-what interest. When I'm finished, I return to the counter. 'I'm done.'

'Now,' she takes my paperwork and shows me a photograph, 'please verify this is your friend.'

The face in the photo is a bull ready to charge. Anthony's eyes and chin flare beneath. 'It's him. Now what?'

'Now you wait.'

Shit. 'How long? I have to be uptown in twenty minutes.'

'Everyone here has someplace they need to be.'

'Is there a bathroom?'

'There's a deli two blocks up.'

Escape under a dark bruising of clouds. By the time I return, a chair has opened up next to a man with the belly of a pastry chef. Across from him, an elderly couple hold onto each other, their voices turning to static in the blue air. Sit and play the game of patience for a timeless while.

'Jacinda Lewis?'

Approach the bail counter like I'm in on something.

'I'm ready for payment. Sign here and here. If he doesn't show up for his court date, you'll forfeit this money.'

'I know. When will he be released?'

'With any luck, he'll be sleeping in his own bed tonight.'

✳

As soon as I settle onto my bar stool, Brian enters Alat's. Shitty fuck. Do I need to start drinking someplace else?

'Hey woman.' He strides over.

Cock block him by putting my purchases on the stool beside me. 'Hi Brian.'

He signals Alat. 'One more for the lady and I'll have a Brooklyn. What's in the bag?'

'A pair of shoes.' For flamenco classes. I want to learn the dance of outcasts.

'Just one? Thought you ladies bought in bulk.'

'I see your carpet burns have healed.'

'Yeah.' He strokes his face before loosening his stockbroker collar. 'Thank you for the other night.' The way he says "other night" has sex in it.

'Don't mention it.' Really. Don't.

'I stopped by last week to return the favor, but you weren't here.'

'You already have. You helped with my math.'

'At least let me take you to dinner.'

'That's okay.'

'Jax, I can take a hint, so relax. I'm not going to hit on you. You look like you could use a friend.' Brian takes on a different hue.

Move my shopping bags to the floor so Brian can sit down. 'Can I trade dinner for some more math help?'

'Sure. When are you taking your test?'

'In three weeks if I feel ready.'

'Are you ready?'

'Why does everything you say sound like a come on?'

'Maybe you have a dirty mind.'

'See?' You can take the boy out of Wall Street, but you can't take Wall Street out of the boy. 'By the way, what happened with your job?'

'The company and I decided to part ways. I've moved on to Goldman Sachs.'

'That was fast. Congratulations. I hear they're too big to fail.'

'Thanks. Yeah, it won't matter if I lose another shit ton of money.'

'I didn't mean it like that. How do you like it there?'

'It works for now. What's your math question?'

Open my text book. 'All of it. I need you to debunk the world of quadrilaterals because I skipped class today. Don't look at me like that. I had good reason.'

'Sure you did.'

'I'll have you know, when I was a model, I was never a no-show. That's one reason clients liked working with me.' Beneath the designers' creations, my body would tell their stories.

'Why don't you become an agent? Then you wouldn't need to take that test.'

Being an agent would break my heart. 'I'm taking the test for me.'

'Then what?'

'No fucking idea.'

'What about becoming a photographer?'

'Cliché. What about you? You said, "It works for now." What's for later?'

'I have a certain figure in mind, and when I hit it, I'll do something different.'

'What?'

Brian looks around the bar as if something interesting is happening elsewhere.

'Come on. I'm curious. What else are Wall Streeters interested in besides hookers and blow?'

'You forgot the dough.'

'Goes without saying.' Wait a beat. 'Fine. Don't tell me. I was only asking to be polite.' Make a show of consulting my textbook. Jesus Christ, he's such a child!

'I want to make furniture.'

'How degenerate.'

'I want to go to Denmark and study to be a master carpenter.'

'Really? That's cool.' Didn't see that coming.

'You think so?'

'Yeah, now I almost want to have dinner with you.'

'What about you? Any secret dreams from childhood?'

'I'm lucky.' Blink hard. 'I already lived mine.'

✳

A Books on Wheels sets up at the St. Nicholas Playground. Upon yellow taxi-colored cubes sit neighborhood kids reading books or drawing. A little girl refuses to share a book with her brother, and the children's mother slaps the girl hard, her cheek reddening into a handprint. A rogue tear drizzles down a face full of hurt. Everyone becomes ten times quieter as the air around the mobile library thickens. The mother pulls her children up, stranding the coveted book on the ground, and drags the boy and girl away. Shame follows the woman up the avenue into traffic.

Head west from the park to class. On my way, I stop at Starbucks for a peace offering. Inside the classroom, Anthony is already seated at his desk, dutifully ignoring my entrance. Sit down next to him and place a selection of Starbucks Petites in front of him.

'I'm not sure those bourgie pops are going to do much for my appetite. Especially since I've been hungry since yesterday.'

'Anthony, I'm sorry I blew off class yesterday. I had something important to do and had no way to contact you. Can we go after class today?'

'I can't.' Anthony's face cracks. 'And I'm in too much of a good mood to stay mad at you. My brother came home last night.'

Thank God I picked the right one. 'That's incredible. I am so happy for you. What happened?'

'I don't know. Somehow his bail got paid. Lukas must have come through. A true man of his word.' Anthony twists me a look. 'Thanks for introducing him.'

My throat is full of glue and needles. Is this my karmic payback? 'Don't mention it.' Shelter in the crook of my arm. My head rumbles with the thunder of avalanching Lukas's Crate & Barrel bookshelves onto the floor of his Amber-shared love nest. Books bloom open on top of their weak spines. To the beat of a flamenco *siguiriyas*, I stomp on his vintage vinyl collection with blazing footwork. Pull on the mask of a politician to quell the rage inside me. Lift my head. 'How's your brother doing?'

'Right now, he's happy to be free, but who knows? Depends on what happened to him inside. We'll have to wait and see. I'm just glad he's home.'

Keep him away from sturdy appliance cords. Gnaw on my knuckles. Michael Paul enters the classroom and begins. Last night's impromptu math session pays off. Get every one of the homework problems right. In my head, the *siguiriyas* speeds up, morphing into the happy, stamping rhythms of a *solea*. In an alternate reality, Anthony is clapping.

✳

Anthony and I sit side by side at a wine bar, sharing tapas. A current of electricity crackles between us; it's the current of people who are unknown to each other, the current of promise. Our knees touch, drawing our heads closer together until we begin and end each other. I catch a glimpse of us in the mirrored wall behind the polished glasses lining the bar. My heart beats against the bars of my ribcage: my face in reflection is whole. As I run my fingers across my cheek, the rutted turf brings me out of sleep.

Sunlight edges the window blinds, breaking up the darkness. Outside, snow veils the trees like lace valentines. This beauty will either melt or harden into something tired and gray and unwelcome.

A ringing phone interrupts my liquid breakfast. 'I knew you'd call.'

'Had to check on my girl. How you doing?'

'It snowed overnight. I'm going to McCarren before it gets yellowed with dog piss.' Wonder if Gene will let Moxie frolic in the snow. 'How's Rocky Horror?'

'I see you shiver with antici......PATION!'

'I'm glad you're still excited about it.'

'I am. I might stay out here for pilot season.'

'You should. It's a good idea.'

'You should visit.'

'Maybe.' Frieda's LA world is as appealing as sunlight through a bottle of old pee. 'After the TASC.'

'When is it?'

'In ten days. I feel ready.'

We lull into a comfortable silence. The rhythm of Frieda's breath reminds of an even-metered palo. Look down at the Moroccan carpet beneath my tapping feet. 'I can't believe it's been a year,' I say, breaking the intimacy of the moment.

'Girl, I can't believe you survived.'

'Me too.' Now, on to figuring out how to live. 'I didn't tell you. I started flamenco classes.'

'You always knew how to move. Your dancing at the after party of the Victoria's Secret fashion show last year was better than the show itself.'

My last big blowout as a model. 'Hey, proof that God has a sick sense of humor, the new show airs tonight.'

'Are you going to watch it?'

'No.' I have zero desire to visit broken ambition. 'A friend of mine is singing at an open mic, and it's her first one in years.' Outside, fresh snow starts falling, turning the air milky white. 'Last night I dreamt my face was whole.'

'I read a line in a script the other day that made me think of you. It was something like, "Beauty is in the eye you live through".'

'You're beautiful only if someone sees you that way?'

'No, you're beautiful depending on how you see the world.'

'Interesting.' Not.

'I know you don't believe it now, but give it some thought. I've got to go. The first year is behind you. That was the hardest part.'

'You're right. Since I woke up this morning, it's been a cake walk.'

Frieda sighs a paragraph. I'm sure she's smoothing her eyebrow. 'Girl, you try my patience.'

'I love you too. Frieda. Thanks for calling.'

✳

Make my way toward McCarren under a thin winter sun. Sharp air travels through my nostrils to penetrate the whiskey fog cobwebbing the inside of my head. Each breath blows a bit clearer.

Outside the Bedford Avenue L stop, bikes huddle together, locked under a cover of fat snowflakes. Up and down the avenue, metal store grates get tinseled, contriving a pair of Babylonian gates that stretch to the park. I ghost into it, breaking the virgin blanket with my footprints. Stop in a glade of nacreous trees and lie down on the soft flurries cloaking the grass. Sweep my arms and legs up and out along the snow. I pause and listen to the stillness. It's one of those rare moments of silence that can grace New York City. Everything is calm, everything is quiet, and you feel how small you are compared to the city, and how lucky you are to live in it, knowing how quickly she will forget you once you've gone.

ACKNOWLEDGMENTS

Books do not write themselves. I owe many thanks to the people and places who inspired *Moxie*. Thank you New York City; *Moxie* is my love letter to you. Aaron and Richard, you know who you are. Both of you touched my life and I am grateful. Camren, Frieda's sass and charisma are yours. My father, Fred Wolfgang Poppe, Lukas's backstory is yours. I hope you don't mind my borrowing it. Thank you Amy Goodman and *Democracy Now!* I would not have known about Kalief Browder if it weren't for your excellent coverage of stories that matter. Amy, you inspire me every day to be better, write better, and write about issues that matter.

An author gets the words on paper; many other people help in shaping them. Thank you, Tony Clerkson for work-shopping this novel with me. You are a wise and funny writing partner. Thanks to my mother, Donna Poppe, who has an encyclopedic command of language and is the ultimate proofreader. Thanks to Julia Lord for reading several drafts and inspiring story development. Adrian Van Young, your support and critiques were invaluable. To my publisher, Jerry Brennan, thank you for making every word count and checking "writerly writing". Your editing made Moxie a much better read and taught me something new about writing. Thanks to Jaime Harris for making the book cover concept a reality.

One of the best pieces of advice I have ever received is from one of my heroes, Jere Van Dyk: "Live your dreams. Then write about it." Thank you, Jere for allowing me to know you and for encouraging me to go to Iraq and to write. Thank you to The Writers Studio, where I learned how to write, and especially to teachers Lisa Bellamy, Joel Hinman, and Therese Eiben who had to suffer through a lot of my bad writing. Thank you to the University of Glasgow MLitt program, where I continued to grow as a writer and learned how to edit. Finally, thanks to the American University of Iraq, Sulaimani for their support of my work.

ABOUT THE AUTHOR

Alex Poppe is the author of two books of fiction: *Girl, World* by Laughing Fire Press (2017) and *Moxie* by Tortoise Books (2019). *Girl, World* was named a 35 Over 35 Debut Book Award winner, First Horizon Award finalist, Montaigne Medal finalist and was short-listed for the Eric Hoffer Grand Prize. It was also awarded an Honorable Mention in General Fiction from the Eric Hoffer Awards. Her short fiction has been a finalist for Glimmer Train's Family Matters contest, a nominee for the Pushcart Prize and commended for the Baker Prize among others. Her non-fiction was named a Best of the Net nominee (2016), a finalist for Hot Metal Bridge's Social Justice Writing contest, and has appeared in *Bust* and *Bella Caledonia*, among others. She is an academic writing lecturer at the American University of Iraq, Sulaimani and is working on her third book of fiction with support from Can Serrat International Art Residency and Asociación Cultural LINEA DE COSTA DUPLO Artist-in-Residency programs.

ABOUT TORTOISE BOOKS

Slow and steady wins in the end—even in publishing. Tortoise Books is dedicated to finding and promoting quality authors who haven't yet found a niche in the marketplace—writers producing memorable work that will stand the test of time.

CPSIA information can be obtained
at www.ICGtesting.com
Printed in the USA
FSHW021212230619
59337FS